My Name is Lucy Barton

BY ELIZABETH STROUT

My Name is Lucy Barton

A Novel

ELIZABETH STROUT

VIKING
an imprint of
PENGUIN BOOKS

VIKING

UK | USA | Canada | Ireland | Australia
India | New Zealand | South Africa

Viking is part of the Penguin Random House group of companies
whose addresses can be found at global.penguinrandomhouse.com.

First published in the United States of America by Random House, an imprint
and division of Penguin Random House LLC, New York 2016
First published in Great Britain by Viking 2016
011

Copyright © Elizabeth Strout, 2016

Printed in Great Britain by Clays Ltd, St Ives plc

A CIP catalogue record for this book is available from the British Library

ISBN: 978–0–241–24877–5

www.greenpenguin.co.uk

MIX
Paper from
responsible sources
FSC® C018179

Penguin Random House is committed to a
sustainable future for our business, our readers
and our planet. This book is made from Forest
Stewardship Council® certified paper.

For my friend
Kathy Chamberlain

My Name is Lucy Barton

There was a time, and it was many years ago now, when I had to stay in a hospital for almost nine weeks. This was in New York City, and at night a view of the Chrysler Building, with its geometric brilliance of lights, was directly visible from my bed. During the day, the building's beauty receded, and gradually it became simply one more large structure against a blue sky, and all the city's buildings seemed remote, silent, far away. It was May, and then June, and I remember how I would stand and look out the window at the sidewalk below and watch the young women—my age—in their spring clothes, out on their lunch breaks; I could see their heads moving in conversation, their blouses rippling in the breeze. I thought how when I got out of the hospital I would never again walk down the sidewalk without giving thanks for being one of those people, and for many years I did that—I would remember the view from the hospital window and be glad for the sidewalk I was walking on.

To begin with, it was a simple story: I had gone into the hospital to have my appendix out. After two days they gave me food, but I couldn't keep it down. And then a fever arrived. No one could isolate any bacteria or figure out what had gone wrong. No one ever did. I took fluids through one IV, and antibiotics came through another. They were attached to a metal pole on wobbly wheels that I pushed around with me, but I got tired easily. Toward the beginning of July, whatever problem had taken hold of me went away. But until then I was in a very strange state—a literally feverish waiting—and I really agonized. I had a husband and two small daughters at home; I missed my girls terribly, and I worried about them so much I was afraid it was making me sicker. When my doctor, to whom I felt a deep attachment—he was a jowly-faced Jewish man who wore such a gentle sadness on his shoulders, whose grandparents and three aunts, I heard him tell a nurse, had been killed in the camps, and who had a wife and four grown children here in New York City—this lovely man, I think, felt sorry for me, and saw to it that my girls—they were five and six—could visit me if they had no illnesses. They were brought into my room by a family friend, and I saw how their little faces were dirty, and so was their hair, and I pushed my IV apparatus into the shower with them, but they cried out, "Mommy, you're so skinny!" They were really frightened. They sat with me on the bed while I dried their hair with a towel, and then they drew pictures, but with apprehension, meaning that they did not interrupt themselves every minute by saying, "Mommy, Mommy, do you like this? Mommy, look at the dress of my fairy princess!" They said very little, the younger one especially seemed unable to speak, and when I put my arms around her, I saw her lower lip thrust out and her chin tremble; she was a tiny thing, trying so hard to be brave. When they left I did not look out the window to watch them walk away with my friend who had brought them, and who had no children of her own.

My husband, naturally, was busy running the household and also busy with his job, and he didn't often have a chance to visit me. He had told me when we met that he hated hospitals—his father had died in one when he was fourteen—and I saw now that he meant this. In the first room I had been assigned was an old woman dying next to me; she kept calling out for help—it was striking to me how uncaring the nurses were, as she cried that she was dying. My husband could not stand it—he could not stand visiting me there, is what I mean—and he had me moved to a single room. Our health insurance didn't cover this luxury, and every day was a drain on our savings. I was grateful not to hear that poor woman crying out, but had anyone known the extent of my loneliness I would have been embarrassed. Whenever a nurse came to take my temperature, I tried to get her to stay for a few minutes, but the nurses were busy, they could not just hang around talking.

About three weeks after I was admitted, I turned my eyes from the window late one afternoon and found my mother sitting in a chair at the foot of my bed. "Mom?" I said.

"Hi, Lucy," she said. Her voice sounded shy but urgent. She leaned forward and squeezed my foot through the sheet. "Hi, Wizzle," she said. I had not seen my mother for years, and I kept staring at her; I could not figure out why she looked so different.

"Mom, how did you get here?" I asked.

"Oh, I got on an airplane." She wiggled her fingers,

and I knew that there was too much emotion for us. So I waved back, and lay flat. "I think you'll be all right," she added, in the same shy-sounding but urgent voice. "I haven't had any dreams."

Her being there, using my pet name, which I had not heard in ages, made me feel warm and liquid-filled, as though all my tension had been a solid thing and now was not. Usually I woke at midnight and dozed fitfully, or stared wide-awake through the window at the lights of the city. But that night I slept without waking, and in the morning my mother was sitting where she had been the day before. "Doesn't matter," she said when I asked. "You know I don't sleep lots."

The nurses offered to bring her a cot, but she shook her head. Every time a nurse offered to bring her a cot, she shook her head. After a while, the nurses stopped asking. My mother stayed with me five nights, and she never slept but in her chair.

During our first full day together my mother and I talked intermittently; I think neither of us quite knew what to do. She asked me a few questions about my girls, and I answered with my face becoming hot. "They're amazing," I said. "Oh, they're just amazing." About my husband, my mother asked nothing, even though—he told me this on the telephone—he was the one who had called her and asked her to come be with me, who had paid her airfare, who had offered to pick her up at the airport—my mother, who had never been in an airplane before. In spite of her saying she would take a taxi, in spite of her refusal to see him face-to-face, my husband had still given her guidance and money to get to me. Now, sitting in a chair at the foot of my bed, my mother also said nothing about my father, and so I said nothing about him either. I kept wishing she would say "Your father hopes you get better," but she did not.

"Was it scary getting a taxi, Mom?"

She hesitated, and I felt that I saw the terror that must have visited her when she stepped off the plane. But she said, "I have a tongue in my head, and I used it."

After a moment I said, "I'm really glad you're here."

She smiled quickly and looked toward the window.

This was the middle of the 1980s, before cellphones, and when the beige telephone next to my bed rang and it was my husband—my mother could tell, I'm sure, by the pitiful way I said "Hi," as though ready to weep—my mother would quietly rise from her chair and leave the room. I suppose during those times she found food in the cafeteria, or called my father from a pay phone down the hall, since I never saw her eat, and since I assumed my father wondered over her safety—there was no problem, as far as I understood it, between them—and after I had spoken to each child, kissing the phone mouthpiece a dozen times, then lying back onto the pillow and closing my eyes, my mother would slip back into the room, for when I opened my eyes she would be there.

That first day we spoke of my brother, the eldest of us three siblings, who, unmarried, lived at home with my parents, though he was thirty-six, and of my older sister, who was thirty-four and who lived ten miles from my parents, with five children and a husband. I asked if my brother had a job. "He has no job," my mother said. "He spends the night with any animal that will be killed the next day." I asked her what she had said, and she repeated what she had said. She added, "He goes into the Pedersons' barn, and he sleeps next to the pigs that will be taken to slaughter." I was surprised to hear this, and I said so, and my mother shrugged.

Then my mother and I talked about the nurses; my mother named them right away: "Cookie," for the skinny one who was crispy in her affect; "Toothache," for the woebegone older one; "Serious Child," for the Indian woman we both liked.

But I was tired, and so my mother started telling me stories of people she had known years before. She talked in a way I didn't remember, as though a pressure of feeling and words and observations had been stuffed down inside her for years, and her voice was breathy and unselfconscious. Sometimes I dozed off, and when I woke I would beg her to talk again. But she said, "Oh, Wizzle-dee, you need your rest."

"I am resting! Please, Mom. Tell me something. Tell me anything. Tell me about Kathie Nicely. I always loved her name."

"Oh yes. Kathie Nicely. Goodness, she came to a bad end."

We were oddities, our family, even in that tiny rural town of Amgash, Illinois, where there were other homes that were run-down and lacking fresh paint or shutters or gardens, no beauty for the eye to rest upon. These houses were grouped together in what was the town, but our house was not near them. While it is said that children accept their circumstances as normal, both Vicky and I understood that we were different. We were told on the playground by other children, "Your family stinks," and they'd run off pinching their noses with their fingers; my sister was told by her second-grade teacher—in front of the class—that being poor was no excuse for having dirt behind the ears, no one was too poor to buy a bar of soap. My father worked on farm machinery, though he was often getting fired for disagreeing with the boss, then getting rehired again, I think because he was good at the work and would be needed once more. My mother took in sewing: A handpainted sign, where our long driveway met the road, announced SEWING AND ALTERATIONS. And though my father, when he said our prayers with us at night, made us thank God that we had enough food, the fact is I was often ravenous, and what we had for supper many nights was molasses on bread. Telling a lie and wasting food were always things to be punished for. Otherwise, on occasion and without warning, my parents—and it was usually my mother and usually in the presence of our father—struck us impulsively and vigorously, as I think some people may have suspected by our splotchy skin and sullen dispositions.

And there was isolation.

We lived in the Sauk Valley Area, where you can go for a long while seeing only one or two houses surrounded by fields, and as I have said, we didn't have houses near us. We lived with cornfields and fields of soybeans spreading to the horizon; and yet beyond the horizon was the Pedersons' pig farm. In the middle of the cornfields stood one tree, and its starkness was striking. For many years I thought that tree was my friend; it was my friend. Our home was down a very long dirt road, not far from the Rock River, near some trees that were windbreaks for the cornfields. So we did not have any neighbors nearby. And we did not have a television and we did not have newspapers or magazines or books in the house. The first year of her marriage, my mother had worked at the local library, and apparently—my brother later told me this—loved books. But then the library told my mother the regulations had changed, they could only hire someone with a proper education. My mother never believed them. She stopped reading, and many years went by before she went to a different library in a different town and brought home books again. I mention this because there is the question of how children become aware of what the world is, and how to act in it.

How, for example, do you learn that it is impolite to ask a couple why they have no children? How do you set a table? How do you know if you are chewing with your mouth open if no one has ever told you? How do you even know what you look like if the only mirror in the house is a tiny one high above the kitchen sink, or if you have never heard a living soul say that you are pretty, but rather, as your breasts develop, are told by your mother that you are starting to look like one of the cows in the Pedersons' barn?

How Vicky managed, to this day I don't know. We were not as close as you might expect; we were equally friendless and equally scorned, and we eyed each other with the same suspicion with which we eyed the rest of the world. There are times now, and my life has changed so completely, that I think back on the early years and I find myself thinking: It was not that bad. Perhaps it was not. But there are times, too—unexpected—when walking down a sunny sidewalk, or watching the top of a tree bend in the wind, or seeing a November sky close down over the East River, I am suddenly filled with the knowledge of darkness so deep that a sound might escape from my mouth, and I will step into the nearest clothing store and talk with a stranger about the shape of sweaters newly arrived. This must be the way most of us maneuver through the world, half knowing, half not, visited by memories that can't possibly be true. But when I see others walking with confidence down the sidewalk, as though they are free completely from terror, I realize I don't know how others are. So much of life seems speculation.

"The thing about Kathie," my mother said, "the thing about Kathie was . . ." My mother leaned forward in her chair and tilted her head with her hand to her chin. Gradually I saw how, in the years since I had last known her, she had gained just enough weight to cause her features to soften; her glasses were no longer black but beige, and the hair beside her face had turned paler, but not gray, so she seemed a slightly larger, fuzzier version of her younger self.

"The thing about Kathie," I said, "is that she was nice."

"I don't know," my mother said. "I don't know how nice she was." We were interrupted by the nurse Cookie, who walked into the room with her clipboard, then held my wrist and took my pulse, gazing into the air, her blue eyes far away. She took my temperature, glanced at the thermometer, wrote something on my chart, and walked out of the room. My mother, who had been watching Cookie, now gazed out the window. "Kathie Nicely always wanted more. I often thought the reason she was friends with me—oh, I don't know if you could call us friends, really, I just sewed for her and she paid me—but I've often thought the reason she would stay and talk—well, she *did* have me over to her place when her troubles arrived—but what I'm trying to say here is that I always thought she *liked* my circumstances being so much lower than her own. She couldn't envy anything about me. Kathie *always* wanted something she didn't have. She had those beautiful daughters, but they weren't enough, she wanted a son. She had that nice house in Hanston, but it wasn't nice enough, she wanted something closer to a city. What city? That's how she was." And then plucking something from her lap, squinting, my mother added in a lower voice: "She was an only child, I think that had something to do with it, how self-centered they can be."

I felt the cold-hot shock that comes from being struck without warning; my husband was an only child, and my mother had told me long before that such a "condition," as she put it, could only lead to selfishness in the end.

My mother went on: "Well, she was jealous. Not of *me,* of course. But for example, Kathie wanted to travel. And her husband wasn't like that. He wanted Kathie to be content and stay at home and they would live off his salary. He did well, he managed a farm of feed corn, you know. They had a perfectly nice life, anyone would have wanted their life, really. Why, they went to dances at some club! I've not been to a dance since high school. Kathie would come to me and get a new dress made just to go to a dance. Sometimes she brought the girls over, such pretty little things and well behaved. I always remember the first time she brought them over. Kathie said to me, 'May I present the pretty Nicely girls.' And when I started to say, 'Oh, they're lovely indeed,' she said, 'No—that's what they're called at their school, in Hanston, the Pretty Nicely Girls.' Now, how does that feel, I've always wondered. To be known as a Pretty Nicely Girl? Though once," my mother said, in her urgent voice, "I caught one of them whispering to her sisters something about our place smelling funny—"

"That's just kids, Mom," I said. "Kids always think places smell funny."

My mother took her glasses off, breathed on each lens briskly and cleaned them with the cloth of her skirt. I thought how naked her face looked then; I could not stop staring at her naked-looking face. "And then one day, you know, the times changed. People think everyone went foolish in the sixties but it wasn't until the seventies, really." Her glasses returned—her face returned—my mother continued. "Or maybe it took that long for the changes to find their way to our cow patch. But one day Kathie came to visit, and she was giggly and strange—girlish, you know. You'd gone off by then. To—" My mother raised her arm and wiggled her fingers. She did not say "school." She did not say "college." And so I didn't say those words either. My mother said, "Kathie fancied someone she'd met, that was clear to me, though she didn't come out and say so. I had a vision—a *visitation*, it would be more accurate to say; it came to me as I sat there looking at her. And I saw this, and I thought: Uh-oh, Kathie's in trouble."

"And she was," I said.

"And she was."

Kathie Nicely had fallen in love with the teacher of one of her children—who were all three in high school by this time—and she began to see this man secretly. Then she told her husband that she had to realize herself more fully and she couldn't do it trapped by domestic chains. So she moved out, left her husband, her daughters, her house. It wasn't until she called my mother weeping that my mother learned the details. My mother drove to find her. Kathie had rented a small apartment, and she was sitting on a beanbag chair, much skinnier than she used to be, and she confessed to my mother that she had fallen in love, but once she'd moved out of her house the fellow had dropped her. Said he could not continue with what they'd been doing. My mother, having come to this point in the story, raised her eyebrows, as though the puzzlement of this was large but not unpleasant to her. "Anyway, her husband was furious and humiliated and would *not* take her back."

Her husband never took her back. He went for over ten years without even speaking to her. When the oldest girl, Linda, got married straight out of high school, Kathie invited my parents to the wedding, because—my mother surmised—Kathie had no one at the wedding who would speak to her. "That girl got married *so* quickly," my mother said, speaking rapidly now, "people thought she was pregnant, but no child arrived that *I* ever heard about, and she divorced him a year later, and went off to Beloit, I believe, looking for a rich husband and I think I heard she found one." My mother said that at the wedding Kathie kept flitting around, desperately nervous. "It was a sad thing to see. Of course we didn't know a soul, and it was obvious she'd just about hired us to be there. We sat in the chairs—I remember on one wall of the place, you know, it was The Club, that silly fancy place in Hanston, and they had all these Indian arrowheads under glass, why was that, I wondered, who would care about *all* those arrowheads—and Kathie would try and talk to some person and then come right back to us. Even Linda, gussied up in white—and Kathie had not asked me to make the gown, the girl went out and bought it—even this bride-girl hardly gave her mother the time of day. Kathie's lived in a little house a few miles from her husband, ex-husband now, for almost fifteen years. All alone. The girls stayed loyal to their father. I'm surprised, when I think of it, that Kathie was even *allowed* at the wedding. Anyway, he never had anyone else."

"He should have taken her back," I said, tears in my eyes.

"I suppose his pride was hurt." My mother shrugged.

"Well, he's alone now, and she's alone, and one day they're going to die."

"True," my mother said.

I became distraught that day, over the fate of Kathie Nicely, while my mother sat at the foot of my bed. At least I remember it that way. I know that I told my mother—with a lump in my throat and my eyes stinging—that Kathie's husband should have taken her back. I'm quite sure I said, "He'll be sorry. I'm telling you, he will."

And my mother said, "I suspect she's the one who's sorry."

But maybe that wasn't what my mother said.

Until I was eleven years old, we lived in a garage. The garage belonged to my great-uncle who lived in the house next door, and in the garage there was only a trickle of cold water from a makeshift sink. Insulation nailed against the wall held a stuffing like pink cotton candy, but it was fiberglass and could cut us, we were told. I was puzzled by that, and would stare at it often, such a pretty pink thing I could not touch; and I was puzzled to think it was called "glass"; odd to think now how much time it seemed to take up in my head, the puzzle of that pretty pink and dangerous fiberglass we lived right next to every minute. My sister and I slept on canvas cots that were bunk beds, metal poles holding one on top of the other. My parents slept beneath the one window, which looked out over the expanse of cornfields, and my brother had a cot in the far corner. At night I would listen to the humming noise of the little refrigerator; it would go on and off. Some nights moonlight came through the window, other nights it was very dark. In the winter it was cold enough that often I could not sleep, and sometimes my mother heated water on the burner and poured it into the red rubber hot water bottle and let me sleep with that.

When my great-uncle died, we moved into the house and we had hot water and a flush toilet, though in the winter the house was very cold. Always, I have hated being cold. There are elements that determine paths taken, and we can seldom find them or point to them accurately, but I have sometimes thought how I would stay late at school, where it was warm, just to *be* warm. The janitor, with a silent nod, and such a kind expression on his face, always let me into a classroom where the radiators were still hissing and so I did my homework there. Often I might hear the faint echo in the gym of the cheerleaders practicing, or the bouncing of a basketball, or perhaps in the music room the band would be practicing too, but I remained alone in the classroom, warm, and that was when I learned that work gets done if you simply do it. I could see the logic of my homework assignments in a way I could not if I did my work at home. And when my homework was finished, I read—until I finally had to leave.

Our elementary school was not big enough to have a library, but there were books in the classrooms that we could take home and read. In third grade I read a book that made me want to write a book. This book was about two girls and they had a nice mother, and they went to stay in a different town for the summer, and they were happy girls. In this new town there was a girl named Tilly—Tilly!—who was strange and unattractive because she was dirty and poor, and the girls were not nice to Tilly, but the nice mother made them be good to her. This is what I remember from the book: Tilly.

My teacher saw that I loved reading, and she gave me books, even grown-up books, and I read them. And then later in high school I still read books, when my homework was done, in the warm school. But the books brought me things. This is my point. They made me feel less alone. This is my point. And I thought: I will write and people will not feel so alone! (But it was my secret.

Even when I met my husband I didn't tell him right away. I couldn't take myself seriously. Except that I did. I took myself—secretly, secretly—very seriously! I knew I *was* a writer. I didn't know how hard it would be. But no one knows that; and that does not matter.)

Because of the hours I stayed in the warm classroom, because of the reading I did, and because I saw that if you didn't miss a piece of the work the homework made sense—because of these things, my grades became perfect. My senior year, the guidance counselor called me to her office and said that a college just outside of Chicago was inviting me to attend with all expenses paid. My parents did not say much about this, probably out of defense for my brother and sister, who had not had perfect, or even particularly good, grades; neither one went on to school.

It was the guidance counselor who drove me to the college on a blistering hot day. Oh, I loved that place immediately, silently, breathlessly! It seemed huge to me, buildings everywhere—the lake absolutely enormous to my eyes—people strolling, moving in and out of classrooms. I was terrified, but not as much as I was excited. I learned rapidly to imitate people, to try to have the gaps in my knowledge about popular culture be unnoticed, although it was not easy, that part.

But I remember this: When I came home for Thanksgiving, I could not fall asleep that night, and it was because I was afraid I had dreamed my life at the college. I was afraid that I would wake and find myself once more in this house and I would be in this house forever, and it seemed unbearable to me. I thought: *No.* I kept thinking that for a long time, until I fell asleep.

Near the college, I got a job, and I bought clothes in a thrift shop; it was the mid-seventies, and clothes like that were acceptable even if you were not poor. To my knowledge, no one spoke of how I dressed, but once, before I met my husband, I fell very much in love with a professor and we had a brief affair. He was an artist and I liked his work, though I understood that I did not understand it, but it was *him* I loved, his harshness, his intelligence, his awareness that certain things had to be forgone if he was to have the life he could have—like children, they were forgone. But I record this now for one purpose alone: He was the only person I remember from my youth as mentioning my clothes, and he mentioned them by comparing me to a woman professor in his department who dressed expensively and was physically large—as I was not. He said, "You have more substance, but Irene has more style." I said, "But style *is* substance." I didn't know yet that such a thing was true;

I had simply written it down one day in my Shakespeare class because the Shakespeare professor had said it and I thought it sounded true. The artist replied, "In that case, Irene has more substance." I was slightly embarrassed for him, that he would think of me as having no style, because the clothes I wore were *me,* and if they came from thrift shops and were not ordinary outfits, it did not occur to me that this would mean anything, except to someone rather shallow. And then he mentioned one day, "Do you like this shirt? I got this shirt at Bloomingdale's once when I was in New York. I'm always impressed with that fact whenever I put it on." And again I felt embarrassed. Because he seemed to think this mattered, and I had thought he was deeper than that, smarter than that; he was an artist! (I loved him very much.) He must have been the first person I remember as wondering about my social class—though at the time I would not have even had words for that— because he would drive me around neighborhoods and say, "Is your house like that?" And the houses he pointed to were never like any house familiar to me, they were not large houses, they just weren't at all like the garage I grew up in, which I had told him about, and they were not like my great-uncle's house either. I was not sorry about the fact of that garage—not in the way I think he meant me to be—but he seemed to think I would be sorry. Still, I loved him. He asked what we ate when I was growing up. I did not say, "Mostly molasses on bread." I did say, "We had baked beans a lot." And he said, "What did you do after that, all hang around and fart?" Then I understood I would never marry him. It's funny how one thing can make you realize something like that. One can be ready to give up the children one always wanted, one can be ready to withstand remarks about one's past, or one's clothes, but then—a tiny re-mark and the soul deflates and says: Oh.

I have since been friends with many men and women and they say the same thing: Always that telling detail. What I mean is, this is not just a woman's story. It's what happens to a lot of us, if we are lucky enough to hear that detail and pay attention to it.

Looking back, I imagine that I was very odd, that I spoke too loudly, or that I said nothing when things of popular culture were mentioned; I think I responded strangely to ordinary types of humor that were un-known to me. I think I didn't understand the concept of irony at all, and that confused people. When I first met my husband William, I felt—and it was a surprise—that he really did understand something in me. He was

the lab assistant to my biology professor my sopho-
more year, and had his own solitary view of the world.
My husband was from Massachusetts, and he was the
son of a German prisoner of war who had been sent to
work the potato fields of Maine. Half starved, as they
often were, this man had won the heart of a farmer's
wife, and when he returned to Germany after the war,
he thought about her and wrote her and told her he was
disgusted with Germany and all they had done. He returned to Maine and ran off with this farmer's wife and
they went to Massachusetts, where he trained to become a civil engineer. Their marriage, naturally, cost
the wife a great deal. My husband had the blond German looks I saw from photos of his father. His father
spoke German a great deal when William was growing
up; though when William was fourteen, his father died.
No letters remain between William's father and mother;
whether his father really felt disgust for Germany, I
don't know. William believed he did, and so for many
years I believed that too.

William, running from the neediness of his widowed
mother, went to school in the Midwest, but when I met
him he was already eager to get back East as soon as he
could. Still, he wanted to meet my parents. This was his

idea, that we would go together to Amgash and he would explain to them how we were going to be married and move to New York City, where he had a post-doctoral appointment waiting for him at a university. In truth it had not occurred to me to worry; I had no concept of turning my back on anything. I was in love, and life was moving forward, and that felt natural. We drove past acres of soybeans and corn; it was early June, and the soybeans were on one side, a sharp green, lighting up the slighting sloping fields with their beauty, and on the other side was the corn, not yet as high as my knees, a bright green that would darken in the coming weeks, the leaves supple now, then becoming stronger. (O corn of my youth, you were my friend!—running and running between the rows, running as only a child, alone, in summer can run, running to that stark tree that stood in the midst of the cornfield—) In my memory the sky was gray as we drove, and it appeared to rise—not clear, but rise—and it was very beautiful, the sense of it rising and growing lighter, the gray having the slightest touch of blue, the trees full with their green leaves.

I remember my husband saying he had not expected my house to be so small.

———

We did not stay with my parents an entire day. My father was wearing his mechanic's coveralls, and he looked at William, and when they shook hands I saw in my father's face great contortions, the kind that frequently preceded what as a child I had called—to myself—the *Thing*, meaning an incident of my father becoming very anxious and not in control of himself. After that, I think that my father did not look at William again, but I can't be sure. William offered to take my parents and my brother and sister into town to eat dinner at some place of their choice. My face felt as hot as the sun when he said that; we had never once eaten in a restaurant as a family. My father told him, "Your money is no good here," and William looked at me with an expression of confusion and I gave my head a tiny shake; I murmured that we should leave. My mother walked out to where I was standing alone by the car and said, "Your father has a lot of trouble with German people. You should have told us."

"Told you?"

"You know your father was in the war, and some German men tried to kill him. He's been having a terrible time from the moment he saw William."

"I know Daddy was in the war," I said. "But he never talked about any of that."

"There are two kinds of men when it comes to their war experience," my mother said. "One talks of it, one doesn't. Your father belongs to the group who doesn't."

"And why is that?"

"Because it wouldn't be decent," my mother said. Adding, "Who in God's name brought you up?"

It was not until many years later, long after, that I learned from my brother how my father, in a German town, had come upon two young men who startled him, and my father had shot them in the back, he did not think they were soldiers, they were not dressed like soldiers, but he had shot them, and when he kicked one over he saw how young he was. My brother told me that William had seemed to my father an older version of this person, a young man who had come back to taunt him, to take away his daughter. My father had murdered two German boys, and as my father lay dying he told my brother that not a day had gone by when he did not think of them, and feel that he should have taken his own life in exchange. What else happened to my father in the war I do not know, but he was in the Battle of the Bulge and he was at the Hürtgen Forest, and these were two of the worst places to be in the war.

My family did not attend my wedding or acknowledge it, but when my first daughter was born I called my parents from New York, and my mother said she had dreamed it, so she already knew I had a baby girl, but she didn't know the name, and she seemed pleased with the name, Christina. After that I called them on their birthdays, and on holidays, and when my other daughter, Becka, was born. We spoke politely but always, I felt, with discomfort, and I did not see any of my family until the day my mother showed up at the foot of my bed in the hospital where the Chrysler Building shone outside the window.

In the dark, I asked my mother quietly if she was awake.

Oh yes, she answered. Quietly. Even though it was only the two of us in this hospital room with the Chrysler Building shining at the window, we still whispered as though someone could be disturbed.

"Why do you think the guy Kathie fell in love with said he couldn't go ahead with it once she left her husband? Did he get scared?"

After a moment my mother said, "I don't know. But Kathie told me he'd confessed to her he was a homo."

"Gay?" I sat up and saw her at the foot of my bed. "He told her he was *gay*?"

"I suppose that's what you call it now. Back then we said 'homo.' He said 'homo.' Or Kathie said it. I don't know who said 'homo.' But he was one."

"Mom, oh, Mom, you're making me laugh," and I could hear she'd started laughing herself, though she said, "Wizzle, I don't really know what's so funny."

"You are." Tears of laughter seeped from my eyes. "The story is. That's a *terrible* story!"

Still laughing—in the same suppressed yet urgent way her talking had been during the day—she said, "I'm not sure what's funny about leaving your husband for a homo gay person and then finding it out, when you think you're going to have a whole man."

"Killing me, Mom." I lay back down.

My mother said, musingly, "I sometimes thought maybe he *wasn't* gay. That Kathie scared him. Leaving her life behind for him. That maybe he made it up."

I considered this. "Back then I don't know if that's the kind of thing a man would make up about himself."

"Oh," said my mother. "Oh, I guess that's true. I honestly don't know about Kathie's fellow. I don't know if he's still around or anything about him at all."

"But did they *do* it?"

"I don't know," my mother answered. "How would I know? Do what? Have intercourse? How in the world would I know?"

"They must've had intercourse," I said, because I thought it was funny saying that, and also because I believed it. "You don't run out on three girls and a husband for a *crush*."

"Maybe you do."

"Okay. Maybe you do." I asked, then, "And Kathie's husband—Mr. Nicely—he really hasn't had anyone since?"

"Ex-husband. Divorced her quick as a bunny. Anyway, I don't believe so. There seems no indication of such a thing. But I suppose you never know."

Maybe it was the darkness with only the pale crack of light that came through the door, the constellation of the magnificent Chrysler Building right beyond us, that allowed us to speak in ways we never had.

"People," I said.

"People," my mother said.

I was so happy. Oh, I was happy speaking with my mother this way!

In those days—and it was the mid-1980s, as I have said—William and I lived in the West Village, in a small apartment near the river. A walk-up, and it was something, with the two small children and having no laundry facilities in the building, and we also had a dog. I would put the younger child in a carry pack on my back—until she got too big—and walk the dog, bending precariously to pick up his mess in a plastic bag, as the signs told one to do: CLEAN UP AFTER YOUR DOG. Always calling out to my older girl to wait for me, not to step off the sidewalk. *Wait, wait!*

I had two friends, and I was half in love with one of them, Jeremy. He lived on the top floor of our building and he was almost, but not quite, the age of my father. He had come originally from France, from the aristocracy, and he gave that all up to be in America, starting as a young man. "Everyone different wanted to be in New York back then," he told me. "It was the place to come to. I guess it still is." Jeremy had decided in the middle of his life to become a psychoanalyst, and when I met him he still had a few patients, but he would not talk to me about what that was like. He had an office across from the New School, and three times a week he went there. I would pass him on the street, and the sight of him—tall, thin, dark-haired, wearing a dark suit, and his soulful face—always made my heart rise. "Jeremy!" I would say, and he would smile and lift his hat in a way that was courtly and old-fashioned and European—this is how I saw it.

His apartment I had seen only once, and this was when I got locked out and had to wait for the super to show up. Jeremy found me on the front stoop with the dog and both children, and I was frantic, and he had me come in. The children were immediately quiet and very well behaved once we got inside his place, as though they knew no children were ever there, and in fact I had never seen children going into Jeremy's apartment.

Only a man or two, or sometimes a woman. The apartment was clean and spare: A stalk of purple iris was in a glass vase against a white wall, and there was art on the walls that made me understand then how far apart he and I were. I say this because I didn't understand the art; they were dark and oblong pieces, almost-abstract-but-not-quite constructions, and I understood only that they were symptoms of a sophisticated world I could never understand. Jeremy was uncomfortable having my family in his place, I could sense that, but he was an exquisite gentleman, and this was why I loved him so.

Three things about Jeremy:

I was standing one day on the front stoop, and as he came out of the building I said, "Jeremy, sometimes when I stand here, I can't believe I'm really in New York City. I stand here and think, Whoever would have guessed? Me! I'm living in the City of New York!"

And a look went across his face—so fast, so involuntary—that was a look of real distaste. I had not yet learned the depth of disgust city people feel for the truly provincial.

——

The second thing about Jeremy: I had my first story published right after I moved to New York, and then it was a while, and my second story was published. On the steps one day, Chrissie told this to Jeremy. "Mommy got a story in a magazine!" He turned to look at me; he looked at me deeply; I had to look away. "No, no," I said. "Just a silly little really small literary magazine." He said, "So—you're a writer. You're an artist. I work with artists, I know. I guess I've always known that about you."

I shook my head. I thought of the artist from college, his knowledge of himself, his ability to forgo children.

Jeremy sat down beside me on the stoop. "Artists are different from other people."

"No. They're not." My face flushed. I had always been different; I did not want to be any more different!

"But they are." He tapped my knee. "You must be ruthless, Lucy."

Chrissie jumped up and down. "It's a sad story," she said. "I can't read yet—I can read *some* words—but it's a sad story."

"May I read it?" Jeremy asked me this.

I said no.

I told him I could not bear it if he didn't like it. He nodded and said, "Okay, I won't ask again. But, Lucy," he said, "you talk to me a lot, and I can't imagine reading anything by you that I wouldn't like."

I remember clearly that he said "ruthless." He did not seem ruthless, and I did not think I was or could be ruthless. I loved him; he was gentle.

He told me to be ruthless.

One more thing about Jeremy: The AIDS epidemic was new. Men walked the streets, bony and gaunt, and you could tell they were sick with this sudden, almost biblical-seeming plague. And one day, sitting on the stoop with Jeremy, I said something that surprised me. I said, after two such men had just walked slowly by, "I know it's terrible of me, but I'm almost jealous of them. Because they have each other, they're tied together in a real community." And he looked at me then, and with real kindness on his face, and I see now that he recognized what I did not: that in spite of my plenitude, I was lonely. Lonely was the first flavor I had tasted in my life, and it was always there, hidden inside the crevices of my mouth, reminding me. He saw this that day, I think. And he was kind. "Yes" is all he said. He could easily have said, "Are you crazy, they're dying!" But he did not say that, because he understood that loneliness about me. This is what I want to think. This is what I think.

In one of those clothing shops New York is famous for, one of those places privately owned and sort of like the art galleries of Chelsea, I found a woman who turned out to affect me a great deal, who may—in ways I don't understand fully—be the reason I have written this. It was many years ago now, my girls would have been perhaps eleven and twelve. In any event, I saw this woman in this clothing store and I felt certain she hadn't seen me. She had the sort of ditzy look you seldom see on women anymore, and she was attractive with it, wore it very well, and she was I would have said almost fifty years old. She was attractive in many ways, stylish, and her hair—ash is the color we used to call it—was well done, by which I mean I understood the color to have come not from a bottle but from the hands of a person trained to work in a salon. And yet it was her face I was drawn to. Her face, which I watched in the mirror while I tried on a black jacket, and finally I said, "Do you think this works?" Her look was surprised, as though she had no idea someone would ask her opinion on clothes. "Oh, I don't work here, I'm sorry," she said. I told her I understood that, I only wanted her opinion. I told her I liked the way she dressed.

"Oh, okay. You *do*? Well, thanks, wow. Yeah, okay. Oh yeah"—she must have seen me tugging on the lapels of the jacket I had asked her about—"it's nice, that *is* nice, are you going to wear it with that skirt?" We discussed the skirt, and whether or not I owned a longer skirt, just in case, as she put it, I "might want to wear heels, you know, a little pickup."

She was as beautiful as her face, I thought, and I loved New York for this gift of endless encounters. Perhaps I saw the sadness in her too. This is what I felt when I got home and her face went through my mind; it would be something you didn't know you saw at the time, as she smiled a great deal and it made her face sparkle. She had the look of a woman who had men still falling in love with her.

I said, "What do you do?"

"For a job?"

"Yes," I said. "You just look like you do something interesting. Are you an actress?" I put the jacket back on the hanger; I did not have the money to buy such a thing.

Oh no, no, she said, and then she said, and I swear I saw her color rise, "I'm just a writer. That's all." As though she might as well confess, because—I sensed— she had been caught before. Or perhaps being "just a writer" was all she thought it was. I asked her what she wrote, and then her color clearly did rise, and she waved her hand and said, "Oh, you know, books, fiction, things like that, it doesn't matter, really."

I had to ask her name, and again I had the sense I'd caused her great embarrassment—she said in one breath: "Sarah Payne"—and I didn't want to cause her embarrassment, so I thanked her for her advice, and she seemed to relax and we spoke of where to get the best shoes—she was wearing a pair of black patent leather high heels—and that made her happy, I thought, and then we parted, each of us saying how nice it had been to meet the other.

———

At home in our apartment—we had moved by then to Brooklyn Heights—and as the children ran about, shouting where was the hair dryer, or the blouse that had been in the laundry?, I looked through our bookshelves and I saw that Sarah Payne looked only a little bit like her jacket photo; I had read her books. And then I remembered being at a party with a man who knew her. He spoke of her work, saying that she was a good writer, but that she could not stop herself from a "softness of compassion" that revolted him, that, he felt, weakened her work. Still, I liked her books. I like writers who try to tell you something truthful. I also liked her work because she had grown up on a rundown apple orchard in a small town in New Hampshire, and she wrote about the rural parts of that state, she wrote about people who worked hard and suffered and also had good things happen to them. And then I realized that even in her books, she was not telling *exactly* the truth, she was always staying away from something. Why, she could barely say her name! And I felt I understood that too.

In the hospital that next morning—now so many years ago—I told my mother I was worried about her not sleeping, and she said that I shouldn't worry about her not sleeping, that she had learned to take catnaps all of her life. And then, once more, there began that slight rush of words, the compression of feeling that seemed to push up through her as she started, that morning, to suddenly speak of her childhood, how she had taken catnaps throughout her childhood too. "You learn to, when you don't feel safe," she said. "You can always take a catnap sitting up."

I know very little about my mother's childhood. In a way, I think this is not unusual—to know little of our parents' childhoods. I mean, in a *specific* way. There is now a large interest in ancestry, and that means names and places and photos and court records, but how do we find out what the daily fabric of a life was? I mean, when the time comes that we care. The Puritanism of my ancestors has not made use of conversation as a source of pleasure, the way I have seen other cultures do. But that morning in the hospital my mother seemed pleased enough to speak of the summers she had gone to live on a farm—she *had* spoken of that in the past. For whatever reasons, my mother spent most of her childhood summers on the farm owned by her Aunt Celia, a woman I have remembered only as a thin, pale person, and whom I, as well as my brother and sister, called "Aunt Seal"—at least in my head I always thought that was who she was, "Aunt Seal," and there was confusion about that, because children are literal thinkers and I had no idea why she would be named after an animal from the ocean I had never seen. She was married to Uncle Roy, who was, as far as I knew, a very nice man. My mother's cousin Harriet was their only child, and her name was the one that came up periodically throughout my youth.

"I was thinking," my mother said, in her soft, rushed

voice, "how one morning, oh, we must have been little, maybe I was five, and Harriet three, I was thinking how we decided to help Aunt Celia take the deadheads off the lemon lilies that grew by the barn. But of course Harriet was just a little thing, and she thought the big buds were the dead parts to take off, and there she was, snapping them right off, when Aunt Celia came out."

"Was Aunt Seal mad?" I asked.

"No, I don't remember that. But I was," my mother said. "I'd tried to tell her what was a bud and what wasn't. Stupid child."

"I never knew Harriet was stupid, you never said she was stupid."

"Well, maybe she wasn't. She probably wasn't. But she was afraid of everything, she was *so* afraid of lightning. She would go hide under the bed and whimper," my mother said. "I never understood it. And so frightened of snakes. Such a silly girl, really."

"Mom. *Please* don't say that word again. Please." Already I was trying to sit up and raise my feet. Even now I always feel the need to get my feet up where I can see them, should I hear that word.

"Say what word again? 'Snakes'?"

"*Mom.*"

"For heaven's sake, I don't— All right. All right." She waved a hand, and gave a little shrug as she turned to look out the window. "You've often reminded me of Harriet," she said. "That silly fear of yours. And your ability to feel sorry for any Tom, Dick, or Harry that came along."

I still do not know, even now, what Tom, Dick, or Harry I'd felt sorry for, or when they'd come along. "But I want to hear," I said. I wanted to hear her voice again, her different, rushed voice.

Toothache, the nurse, walked into the room; she took my temperature, but she did not look into space the way Cookie did. Instead Toothache looked at me carefully, then looked at the thermometer, and then told me that the fever was the same as it had been the day before. She asked my mother if she wanted anything, and my mother shook her head quickly. For a moment Toothache stood, her woebegone face seeming at a loss. Then she measured my blood pressure, which was always fine, and it was fine that morning. "All right, then," said Toothache, and both my mother and I thanked her. She wrote a few things on my chart, and at the door she turned to say that the doctor would be in soon.

"The doctor seemed like a nice man," my mother said, addressing the window. "When he came in last night."

Toothache glanced back at me as she left.

After a moment I said, "Mom, tell me more about Harriet."

"Well, you know what happened to Harriet." My mother returned to the room, to me.

I said, "But you always *liked* her though, right?"

"Oh, sure—what was there not to like about Harriet? She had that *very* poor luck with her marriage. She married a man from a couple towns away she met at a dance, a square dance in a barn, I think, and people were pleased for her, you know, she wasn't a great deal to look at even back then in the prime of her youth."

"What was wrong with her?" I asked.

"Nothing was wrong with her. She was just always fretful, even as a young girl, and she had those buck teeth. And she smoked, which gave her bad breath. But she was a sweet thing, she was that, never meant harm to anyone, and she had those two kids, Abel and Dottie—"

"Oh, I loved Abel when I was a kid," I said.

"Yes, Abel was just a wonderful person always.

Funny how that can happen, out of nowhere a tree rises up strong, and that's what he was. Anyway, one day Harriet's husband went out to get her cigarettes and—"

"Never came back," I finished.

"I should *say* he never came back. I should *say* he indeed never came back. He dropped dead on the street, and Harriet had such a time trying to keep the state from taking those kids. He left her nothing, poor woman, I'm sure he didn't expect to just *die*. They were living in Rockford by then—you know, it's over an hour away—and she stayed there, I never knew why. But she would send the kids to us a few weeks each summer, once we were in the house. Oh, such sad-looking children. I'd always try and make Dottie a new dress to send her home with."

Abel Blaine. His pants were too short, above his ankles, I remember, and kids laughed at him when we went into town, and he always smiled as though none of it mattered. His teeth were crooked and bad, but otherwise he was nice-looking; perhaps he knew that he was nice-looking. I think, really, his heart was just good. He was the one who taught me to search for food from the dumpster behind Chatwin's Cake Shoppe. What was striking was the lack of furtiveness he displayed as he stood in the dumpster and tossed aside boxes until he found what he was looking for—the old cakes and rolls and pastries from days before. Neither Dottie nor my own sister and brother were ever with us, I don't know where they were. After a few visits to Amgash, Abel did not come back; he had a job as an usher in a theater where he lived. He sent me one letter, and enclosed a brochure that showed the theater's lobby; it was just beautiful, I remember, with many different colored tiles, ornate and gorgeous.

"Abel landed on his feet," my mother told me.

"Tell me again," I said.

"He managed to marry the daughter of someone he worked for; the boss's-daughter story, I guess, is his story. He lives in Chicago, has for years," my mother said. "His wife's quite a hoity-toity and won't have anything to do with poor Dottie, whose husband ran off with someone else a few years ago now. He was from the East, Dottie's husband. You know."

"No."

"Well." My mother sighed. "He was. Somewhere here along the Eastern Seaboard he came from—" My mother gave a small toss of her head toward the window as though to indicate this was where Dottie's husband came from. "Thought he was just a tiny bit better than she was, probably. Wizzle, how can you live with no *sky*?"

"There's sky." But I added, "Except I know what you mean."

"But how can you live without sky?"

"There's people instead," I said. "So tell me why."

"Why what?"

"Why did Dottie's husband run off?"

"How do I know? Oh, I guess I do know. He met some woman at the local hospital when he had his gallbladder out. Say, that's almost like you!"

"Like me? You think I'm going to run off with Cookie or Serious Child?"

"You never know what attracts people to each other," my mother answered. "But I don't think he ran off with any Toothache." My mother tilted her head in the direction of the door. "Though he may have run off with a child, I'm sure she's not a *serious* child, you know, I mean—" My mother leaned forward to whisper, "Dark or whatever ours is, you know, Indian." My mother sat back. "But I'm rather sure she's younger than Dottie and more attractive. He left Dottie the house they lived in, and she's turned it into a bed-and-breakfast. Doing all right, as far as I know. And Abel's in Chicago doing more than all right, so good for poor Harriet after all. Well, I suppose she'd worried about Dottie. My word, Harriet worried about everyone. Not worrying now, though, I guess. She's been dead for years. Like that, in her sleep one night. Not a bad way to go."

I dozed on and off listening to my mother's voice.

I thought: All I want is this.

But it turned out I wanted something else. I wanted my mother to ask about my life. I wanted to tell her about the life I was living now. Stupidly—it was just stupidity—I blurted out, "Mom, I got two stories published." She looked at me quickly and quizzically, as if I had said I had grown extra toes, then she looked out the window and said nothing. "Just dumb ones," I said, "in tiny magazines." Still she said nothing. Then I said, "Becka doesn't sleep through the night. Maybe she gets it from you. Maybe she'll take catnaps too." My mother kept looking out the window.

"But I don't want her to not feel safe," I added. "Mom, why didn't you feel safe?"

My mother closed her eyes as though the very question might drop her into a nap, but I did not think for one minute she had gone to sleep.

After many moments she opened her eyes and I said to her, "I have a friend, Jeremy. He used to live in France, and his family was part of the aristocracy."

My mother looked at me, then looked out the window, and it was a long time before she said, "So he says," and I said, "Yes, so he says," in a tone of apology, and in a way that let her know we need not discuss him—or my life—any further.

Right then, through my doorway, came the doctor. "Girls," he said, and nodded. He went and shook my mother's hand, as he had the day before. "How's everyone today?" Immediately he swooshed the curtain around me and this separated me from my mother. I loved him for many reasons, and one reason was for that: how he made his visits private for the two of us. I could hear my mother's chair move, and I knew she'd left the room. The doctor held my wrist to take my pulse, and when he gently lifted my hospital gown, in order to check the scar, as he did each day, I watched his hands, thick-fingered and lovely, his plain gold wedding band glinting, pressing gently on the area near the scar, and he looked into my face to see if it hurt. He asked by raising his eyebrows, and I'd shake my head. The scar was healing nicely. "Healing nicely," he said, and I said, "Yes, I know." And we'd smile because it seemed to mean something—that it was not the scar trying to keep me sick. The smile was our acknowledgment of *something,* is what I mean. I have always remembered this man, and for years I gave money to that hospital in his name. And I thought then, and I think now, still, of the phrase "the laying on of hands."

The truck. At times it comes to me with a clarity I find astonishing. The dirt-streaked windows, the tilt of the windshield, the grime on the dashboard, the smell of diesel gas and rotting apples, and dogs. I don't know, in numbers, how many times I was locked in the truck. I don't know the first time, I don't know the last time. But I was very young, probably no more than five years old the last time, otherwise I'd have been in school all day. I was put there because my sister and brother were in school—this is my thought now—and my parents were both working. Other times I was put there as punishment. I remember saltine crackers with peanut butter, which I couldn't eat because I was so frightened. I remember pounding on the glass of the windows, screaming. I did not think I would die, I don't think I thought anything, it was just terror, realizing that no one was to come, and watching the sky get darker, and feeling the cold start in. Always I screamed and screamed. I cried until I could hardly breathe. In this city of New York, I see children crying from tiredness, which is real, and sometimes from just crabbiness, which is real. But once in a while I see a child crying with the deepest of desperation, and I think it is one of the truest sounds a child can make. I feel almost, then, that I can hear within me the sound of my own heart breaking, the way you could hear outside in the open air—when the conditions were exactly right—the corn growing in the fields of my youth. I have met many people, even from the Midwest, who tell me that you cannot hear the corn growing, and they are wrong. You cannot hear my heart breaking, and I know that part is true, but to me, they are inseparable, the sound of growing corn and the sound of my heart breaking. I have left the subway car I was riding in so I did not have to hear a child crying that way.

My mind went very strange places during these episodes of being in the truck. I thought I saw a man coming toward me, I thought I saw a monster, I thought one time I saw my sister. Then I would calm myself, and say aloud to myself, "It's okay, sweetie. A nice woman's going to come soon. And you're a very good girl, you're such a good girl, and she's a relative of Mommy's and she'll need you to go live with her because she's lonely and wants to have a nice little girl to live with." I would have this fantasy, and it was very real to me, it kept me calm. I dreamed of not being cold, of having clean sheets, clean towels, a toilet that worked, and a sunny kitchen. I allowed myself into heaven this way. And then the cold would come in, and the sun would go down, and my crying would start again, as a whimper, then more forcefully. And then my father would show up, unlock the door, and sometimes he carried me. "No reason to cry," he sometimes said, and I can remember the feel of his warm hand spread against the back of my head.

The doctor, who wore his sadness with such loveliness, had come to check on me the night before. "I had a patient on another floor," he said. "Let me see how you're doing." And he swished the curtain around me as he always did. He didn't take my temperature with a thermometer but held his hand to my forehead, and then took my pulse with his fingers to my wrist. "Okay, then," he said. "Sleep well." He made a fist and kissed it, then held it in the air as he unswished the curtain and left the room. For many years, I loved this man. But I have already said that.

Other than Jeremy, the only friend I had in the Village during this time in my life was a tall Swedish woman named Molla; she was at least ten years older than I, but she also had small children. She passed by our door one day with her kids on the way to the park, and she started talking to me right away about really personal things. Her mother had not treated her well, she said, and so when she had her first baby she became very sad, and her psychiatrist told her that she was feeling grief because of everything she had not received from her own mother, et cetera. I didn't disbelieve her, but her story wasn't what was interesting to me. It was her style, her forthright spilling out about things I didn't know people spoke of. And she was not really interested in me, which was freeing. She liked me, she was nice to me, she was bossy and told me how to hold my babies and how to get them to the park, and so I liked her back. Mostly she was like watching a movie or something foreign, which of course she was. She made references to movies, and I never knew what she was talking about. She must have noticed this, and she was polite about it, or maybe she did not believe that I could have a blank face when she spoke of Bergman films or television shows from the sixties, or music too. I had no knowledge of popular knowledge, as I have said. At that time, I barely understood that about myself. My husband knew it about me, and would try to help me out if he was around, maybe saying, "Oh, my wife didn't see a lot of movies growing up, don't worry." Or "My wife's parents were strict and never let her watch television." Not giving away my childhood of poverty, because even poor people had TVs. Who would have believed it?

"Mommy," I said softly that next night.

"Yes?"

"Why did you come here?"

There was a pause, as though she was shifting her position in the chair, but my head was turned toward the window.

"Because your husband called and asked for me to come. He needed you babysat, I believe."

For a long while there was silence, maybe it was ten minutes, maybe it was almost an hour, I really don't know, but finally I said, "Well, thank you anyway," and she did not reply.

In the middle of the night, I woke from a nightmare

I could not remember. Her voice came quietly, "Wizzle-dee, sleep. Or if you can't sleep, just rest. Please rest, honey."

"You're never sleeping," I said, trying to sit up. "How can you go *every* night never sleeping? Mom, it's been two nights!"

"Don't worry about me," she said. She added, "I like your doctor. He's watching out for you. The residents know nothing, how can they? But he's good, he'll see to it that you get better."

"I like him too," I said. "I love him."

A few minutes later she said, "I'm sorry we had so little money when you kids were growing up. I know it was humiliating."

In the dark I felt my face become very warm. "I don't think it mattered," I said.

"Of course it mattered."

"But we're all fine now."

"I'm not so sure." She said this thoughtfully. "Your brother is almost a middle-aged man who sleeps with pigs and reads children's books. And Vicky—she's still mad about it. The kids made fun of you at school. Your father and I didn't know that, I suppose we should have. Vicky's really still pretty mad."

"At you?"

"Yes, I think so."

"That's silly," I said.

"No. Mothers are supposed to protect their children."

After a while I said, "Mom, there are kids with mothers who sell them for drugs. There are kids whose mothers take off for days and just leave them. There are—" I stopped. I was tired of what was sounding untrue.

She said, "You were a different kind of kid from Vicky. And from your brother too. You didn't care as much what people thought."

"What makes you say that?" I asked.

"Well, look at your life right now. You just went ahead and . . . *did* it."

"I see." I didn't see, though. How do we ever see something about our own self? "When I went to school when I was little," I said, lying flat on my back on the hospital bed, the lights from the buildings showing through the window, "I'd miss you all day. I couldn't talk when a teacher called on me, because I had a lump in my throat. I don't know how long it lasted. But I missed you so much, sometimes I'd go into the bathroom to cry."

"Your brother threw up."

I waited for a moment. Many moments went by.

Finally she said, "Every morning before school in fifth grade your brother threw up. I never found out why."

"Mom," I said, "what children's books does he read?"

"The ones about the little girl on the prairie, there's a series of them. He loves them. He's not slow, you know."

I turned my eyes toward the window. The light from the Chrysler Building shone like the beacon it was, of the largest and best hopes for mankind and its aspirations and desire for beauty. That was what I wanted to tell my mother about this building we saw.

I said, "Sometimes I remember the truck."

"The truck?" My mother's voice sounded surprised. "I don't know anything about a truck," she said. "What do you mean, your father's old Chevy truck?"

I wanted to say—oh, terribly I wanted to say: Not even when there was the really, really long brown snake in there with me one time? I wanted to ask her this, but I could not bear to say the word, even now I can barely stand to say the word, and to tell anyone how frightened I was when I saw that I had been locked into a truck with such a long brown— And he moved so quickly. So quickly.

When I was in the sixth grade a teacher arrived from the East. His name was Mr. Haley and he was a young man; he taught us social studies. There are two things I remember about him: The first is that one day I had to go to the bathroom, which I hated to do because it called attention to me. He gave me the pass, nodding once, smiling. When I returned to the room and approached him to return the pass—it was a large block of wood that we were required to hold in the corridor to prove that we had permission to be out of the classroom—when I handed him back the pass, I saw Carol Darr, a popular girl, do something—a kind of hand gesture or something that I knew from experience was making fun of me, and she was doing it toward her friends so they could make fun of me as well. And I remember that Mr. Haley's face became red, and he said: Do not *ever* think you are better than someone, I will not tolerate that in my classroom, there is no one here who is better than someone else, I have just witnessed expressions on the faces of some of you that indicate you think you are better than someone else, and I will not tolerate that in my classroom, I will not.

I glanced at Carol Darr. In my memory she was chastened, she felt bad.

I fell silently, absolutely, immediately in love with this man. I have no idea where he is, if he is still alive, but I still love this man.

The other thing about Mr. Haley was that he taught us about the Indians. Until then I hadn't known that we took their land from them with a deception that caused Black Hawk to rebel. I didn't know that the whites gave them whiskey, that the whites killed their women in their own cornfields. I felt that I loved Black Hawk as I did Mr. Haley, that these were brave and wonderful men, and I could not believe how Black Hawk was taken on a tour of cities after his capture. I read his autobiography as soon as I could. And I remembered the line he said: "How smooth must be the language of the whites, when they can make right look like wrong, and wrong like right." I worried too that his autobiography, which had been transcribed by an interpreter, would not be accurate, and so I wondered, Who is Black Hawk, really? And I got a sense of him as strong, and bewildered, and when he spoke of "our Great Father, the President," he used nice terms, and that made me sad.

All of this, I am saying, made a huge impression on me, the indignities that we had forced onto these people. And when I came home from school one day after we learned how the Indian women planted a field of corn and the white men came and plowed it up, my mother was in front of our garage-home, which we had only recently moved out of, she may have been trying to fix something, I don't recall, but she was squatting by the front door, and I said to her, "Mommy, do you know what we did to the Indians?" I said this slowly and with awe.

My mother wiped at her hair with the back of her hand. "I don't give a damn what we did to the Indians," she said.

———

Mr. Haley left at the end of the year. In my memory he was going into the service, and this could only have been Vietnam, since it was during that time. I have since looked up his name on the Veterans Memorial in Washington, D.C., and it isn't there. I don't know anything more about him, but in my memory Carol Darr was all right to me—in his class—after that. We all liked him, is what I mean. We all respected him. This is no small feat for a man with a classroom of twelve-year-olds to accomplish, but he did.

Over the years I have thought about the books that my mother said my brother was reading. I'd read them too; they hadn't touched me too deeply. As I said, my heart was with Black Hawk and not with these white people who lived on the prairie. And so I have thought about these books: What was it in them that my brother liked? The family of this series was a nice family. They made their way across the prairie, they were sometimes in trouble, but always the mother was kind and the father loved them very much.

My daughter Chrissie has turned out to love these books as well.

———

When Chrissie turned eight, I bought her the book about Tilly that had meant so much to me. Chrissie loved to read; I was happy to have her unwrap this book. She unwrapped it at a birthday party I had for her, and her friend whose father was a musician was there. When he came to pick his daughter up after the party, he stayed and talked, and he mentioned the artist I had known in college. The artist had moved to New York not long after I had. I said that I knew him. The musician said, You're prettier than his wife. No, he said, when I asked. The artist had no children.

A few days later, Chrissie said to me about the book with Tilly in it, "Mom, it's kind of a dumb book."

But the books my brother loved about the girl on the prairie, Chrissie still loves those books too.

On the third day that my mother sat at the foot of my bed, I could see the fatigue on her face. I didn't want her to leave, but she seemed unable to accept the nurses' offer to bring in a cot, and I felt she would leave soon. As has often been the case with me, I began to dread this in advance. I remember my first dreading-in-advance as having to do with the dentist of my childhood. Because we had little dental care in our youth, and because genetically we were thought to have "soft teeth," any trip to the dentist was quite naturally filled with dread. The dentist provided free care in a manner that was ungenerous, both in time and manner, as though he hated us for being who we were, and I worried the entire time once I heard I would have to see him. It was not often that I saw him. But early on I saw this: You are wasting time by suffering twice. I mention this only to show how many things the mind cannot will itself to do, even if it wants to.

It was Serious Child who came for me in the middle of the next night, saying that blood tests had come back from the lab and I needed a CAT scan immediately. "But it's the middle of the night," my mother said. Serious Child said I had to go. And so I said, "Let's go, then," and soon some orderlies showed up and put me on a gurney and I waved my fingers at my mother and they took me into one large elevator after another. It was dark in the hallways, and in the elevators; everything seemed very dim. I had not left my room at night before, I had not seen that night was different than day even in the hospital. After a very long trip and many turns I was pushed into a room and someone put a small tube into my arm and another small tube down my throat. "Hold still," they said. I couldn't even nod.

After a long time—but what I mean by that, I don't know in real time or terms—I was pushed into the CAT scan circle and there were some clicks and then it went dead. "Shit," said a voice behind me. For another long time I lay there. "The machine's broken," the voice said, "but we need this scan or the doctor will kill us." I lay there a long time, and I was very cold. I learned that hospitals are often cold. I was shivering, but no one noticed; I'm sure they would have brought me a blanket. They only wanted the machine to work, and I understood that.

Finally I was pushed through and there were the right-sounding clicks and tiny red lights blinking, and then the tube was taken out of my throat and I was pushed out into the hallway. This is the memory I think I will never forget: My mother was sitting in the dark waiting area there in the deep basement of that hospital, her shoulders slumped slightly in fatigue, but sitting with all the seeming patience in the world. "Mommy," I whispered, and she waved her fingers. "How did you ever find me?"

"Wasn't easy," she said. "But I have a tongue in my head, and I used it."

The next morning, Toothache brought with her the news that the tests had come out all right, that in spite of what had shown up in my blood the CAT scan was okay, the doctor would explain it all later. Toothache had also brought with her a gossip magazine, and she asked my mother if she'd like to read it. My mother shook her head quickly, as though she'd been asked to handle a person's private body parts. "I'd like it," I told Toothache, holding out my hand, and she gave it to me and I thanked her. The magazine lay that morning on my bed. Then I put it into the drawer in my table that had the telephone on it, and I did that—hid it—in case the doctor came in. So I was like my mother, we did not want to be judged by what we read, and while she wouldn't even read such a thing, I only didn't want to be seen with it. This strikes me as odd, so many years later. I was in the hospital, essentially so was she; what better time to read anything that takes the mind away? I had a few books from home near my bed, though I had not read them with my mother there, nor had she looked at them. But about the magazine, I'm sure it would not have made any dent in my doctor's heart. But that is how sensitive we both were, my mother and I. There is that constant judgment in this world: How are we going to make sure we do not feel inferior to another?

It was merely a magazine about movie stars, one my own girls and I, when they were older, would look at for fun if we needed time to go by, and this particular magazine often featured a story about an ordinary person who had suffered something extraordinarily awful. When I took the magazine from the drawer that afternoon, I saw an article about a woman who had gone into a barn in Wisconsin to find her husband one evening and had her arm chopped off—literally chopped with an ax—by a man who had gotten out of the state mental asylum. This happened while her husband, tied to a post by the horse pens, watched. He screamed, which made the horses scream, and I guess the woman must have screamed like crazy—it did not say she passed out—and the sound of such noises caused the escaped-from-the-asylum-man to run off. The woman, who easily could have bled to death as her arteries were spurting blood, managed to call for help, and a neighbor came right over and tied her arm with a tourniquet, and now the husband and wife and neighbor made a point of starting each day by praying together. There was a photo of them in the early morning sun by the barn door in Wisconsin, and they were praying. The woman prayed with her one remaining arm and hand; they were hoping to get her a prosthetic soon, but there was the issue of money. I told my mother I thought it was bad taste to photograph people praying, and she said the entire thing was bad taste.

"He's a lucky husband, though," she said in a few moments. "I see on the news those shows where a man might have to watch his wife be raped."

I put the magazine down. I looked at my mother at the foot of my bed, this woman I had not seen for years. "Seriously?" I asked.

"Seriously what?"

"A man watched his wife be raped? What were you

watching, Mom?" I didn't add what I most wanted to:
And when did you guys get a TV?

"I saw it on television, I just told you that."

"But on the news, or one of those cop show things?"

I saw—I felt I saw—her considering this, and she
said, "The news, one night at Vicky's house. Somewhere
in one of those awful countries." Her eyes flipped shut.

I picked the magazine back up and rustled through
it. I said, "Hey, look—this woman has a pretty gown.
Mom, look at this pretty gown." But she did not re-
spond or open her eyes.

This is how the doctor found us that day. "Girls," he
said, then stopped when he saw my mother with her
eyes closed. He stayed just within the door, he and I
both watching for a moment to see if my mother was
truly asleep or if she would open her eyes. That moment, both of us watching to see, made me recall how
in my youth there were times that I wanted desperately
to run to a stranger when we went into town and say,
"You need to help me, please, please, can you please get
me out of there, bad things are going on—" And yet I
never did, of course; instinctively I knew that no
stranger would help, no stranger would dare to, and
that in the end such a betrayal would make things far

worse. And so now I turned from watching my mother to watching my doctor, for in essence this was the stranger I had hoped for, and he turned and must have seen something on my face, and I—so briefly—felt I saw something on his, and he held up a hand to indicate he'd come back, and when he stepped out, I felt myself dropping into something familiar and dark from long ago. My mother's eyes remained shut for many more minutes. To this day I have no idea if she was sleeping or just staying away from me. I wanted terribly to talk to my little children then, but if my mother was asleep I couldn't wake her by speaking into the phone next to the bed, and also the girls would have been in school.

All day I had wanted to speak to my girls, I could barely stand it, so I pushed my apparatus out into the hallway and asked the nurses if I could make a call from their desk, and they pushed a phone toward me, and I called my husband. I was desperate not to have any tears drip from my eyes. He was at work, and he felt bad for me, hearing how much I missed him and the kids. "I'll call the sitter and have her call you just as soon as they're home. Chrissie has a play date today."

So life goes on, I thought.

(And now I think: It goes on, until it doesn't.)

———

I had to sit in a chair at the nurses' station while I tried not to cry. Toothache put her arm around me, and even now I love her for that. I have sometimes been sad that Tennessee Williams wrote that line for Blanche DuBois, "I have always depended on the kindness of strangers." Many of us have been saved many times by the kindness of strangers, but after a while it sounds trite, like a bumper sticker. And that's what makes me sad, that a beautiful and true line comes to be used so often that it takes on the superficial sound of a bumper sticker.

I was wiping my face with my bare arm when my mother came to find me, and we all—Toothache, myself, the other nurses—waved to her. "I thought you were napping," I said as she and I went back to my room. She said that she had been napping. "The sitter may call soon," I said, and I told her how Chrissie had a play date.

"What's a play date?" my mother asked.

I was glad we were alone. "It just means she's going to someone's house after school."

"Who's the play date with?" my mother asked, and I felt that her asking was her way of being nice after what she must have seen in my face, my sadness.

As we walked down the hallway of the hospital, I told her about Chrissie's friend, how the mother taught fifth grade and the father was a musician but also a jerk, kind of, and they were not happy in their marriage but the girls seemed to like each other a great deal, and my mother nodded throughout all this. When we got back to my room, the doctor was there. His face was businesslike as he swished the curtain and pressed on my scar. He said, brusquely, "About the scare last night: An inflammation was showing up in the blood and we needed the CAT scan. Get your fever down, keep some solid food down, and we can send you home." His voice was different enough that he might have slapped me with each word. I said, "Yes, sir," and did not look at him. I have learned this: A person gets tired. The mind or the soul or whatever word we have for whatever is not just the body gets tired, and this, I have decided, is—usually, mostly—nature helping us. I was getting tired. I think—but I don't know—that he was getting tired too.

———

The sitter called. She was just a young girl, and she kept assuring me that the kids were doing fine. She held the phone to Becka's ear, and I said, "Mommy will be home soon," again and again and again, and Becka didn't cry, so I was happy. "When?" she asked, and I kept saying soon, and that I loved her. "I love you, and you know that, right?" "What?" she asked. "I love you and I miss you and I'm here away from you so I can get well, and I'm going to get well, and then I'll see you very soon, okay, angel?"

"Okay, Mommy," she said.

In the Metropolitan Museum of Art, which sits so large and many-stepped on Fifth Avenue in New York, there is a section on the first floor referred to as the sculpture garden, and I must have walked past this particular sculpture many times with my husband, and with the children as they got older, me thinking only of getting food for the kids, and never really knowing what a person did in a museum of this nature where there were so many things to look at. In the middle of these needs and worries is a statue. And only recently—in the last few years—when the light was hitting it with a splendid wash, did I stop and look at it and say: Oh.

It is a marble statue of a man with his children near

him, and the man has such desperation on his face and the children at his feet appear to be clinging, begging him, while he gazes out toward the world with a tortured look, his hands pulling at his mouth, but his children look only at him, and when I finally saw this, I said inside myself, Oh.

I read the placard, which let me know that these children are offering themselves as food for their father, he is being starved to death in prison, and these children only want one thing—to have their father's distress disappear. They will allow him—oh, happily, happily—to eat them.

And I thought, So that guy knew. Meaning the sculptor. He knew.

And so did the poet who wrote what the sculpture has shown. He knew too.

A few times I made a trip to the museum specifically to see my starving father-man with his children, one grabbing at his leg, and when I got there I didn't know what to do. He was as I had remembered him, and so I stood at a loss. Later I realized I got what I needed when there was a furtiveness to my seeing him, such as if I was in a hurry to meet someone elsewhere, or if I was with someone in the museum and I'd say I needed to use the bathroom, just to get away and see this on my own. But not on my own the same way as when I made the trip entirely alone to see this frightened starving father-man. And he is always there, except for once when he was not. The guard said he was upstairs in a special exhibit and I felt insulted by the whole thing, that others wanted to see him that much!

Pity us.

I thought those words later, as I thought of my response when the guard told me the statue was upstairs. I thought, Pity us. We don't mean to be so small. Pity us—it goes through my head a lot—Pity us all.

"Who *are* these people?" my mother asked.

I was lying on my back facing the window; it was evening, and the lights of the city were starting to come on. I asked my mother what she meant. She answered, "These foolish people in this foolish magazine, I don't know one name of any of them. They all seem to like to have their picture taken getting coffee or shopping, or—" I stopped listening. It was the sound of my mother's voice I most wanted; what she said didn't matter. And so I listened to the sound of her voice; until these past three days it had been a long time since I had heard it, and it was different. Perhaps my memory was different, for the sound of her voice used to grate my nerves.

This sound was the opposite of that—always the sense of compression, the urgency.

"Look at this," my mother said. "Wizzle, look at this. My goodness," she said.

And so I sat up.

She handed me the gossip magazine. "Did you see this?"

I took it from her. "No," I said. "I mean, I saw it, but I didn't care."

"No, but my goodness, I care. Her father was a friend of your father's from a long, long time ago. Elgin Appleby. It says it right here, look at this. 'Her parents, Nora and Elgin Appleby.' Oh, he was a funny man. He could make the Devil laugh."

"Well, the Devil laughs easily," I said, and my mother looked at me. "How did Daddy know him?" It was the only time during her stay with me in the hospital that I remember being angry with her, and this was because she casually spoke of my father that way, after not speaking of him at all, except to mention his truck.

She said, "When they were young. Who knows, but Elgin moved to Maine and worked on a farm there, I don't know why he moved. But look at her, this child, Annie Appleby. Look at her, Wizzle." My mother pointed at the magazine she had handed me. "I think she looks— I don't know." My mother sat back. "What does she look like?"

"Nice?" I didn't think she looked nice; she looked something, but I would not have said "nice."

"No, not nice," said my mother. "Something. She looks something."

I stared at the picture again. She was next to her new boyfriend, an actor from a television series my husband watched some nights. "She looks like she's seen stuff," I finally said.

"That's it," my mother nodded. "You're right, Wizzle. That's what I thought too."

The article was a long one, and it was more about Annie Appleby than the fellow she was with. It said that she'd grown up on a potato farm in the St. John Valley in Aroostook County in Maine, that she had not finished high school, that she had left to join a theater company, and that she missed her home. "Of course I do," Annie Appleby was quoted as saying, "I miss the beauty every day." When asked if she wanted to go into movies instead of staying on the stage, she answered, "Not a bit. I love the audience being right there, although I don't think about them when I'm onstage, I just know what they need, which is for me to be good at my job of acting for them."

I put the magazine down. "She's pretty," I said.

"I didn't think she was pretty," my mother said. It seemed a while before she added, "I think she's more than pretty. She's beautiful. I wonder what it's like for her to be famous." My mother seemed to be pondering this.

Maybe it was because for the first time since she had been here she had mentioned my father, and not just his truck, or maybe it was because she had called someone else's daughter beautiful, but I said with some sarcasm, "I didn't know you ever cared what it felt like for anyone to be famous." Right away I experienced a terrible feeling: This was my mother, who had found her way to the basement just the night before, all the way to the basement of this big awful hospital in the nighttime, she had gone to make sure her daughter was okay, and so I said, "But I've wondered sometimes, because once I saw"—and I named a famous actress—"in Central Park, and she was walking along, and I thought, What is that like?" I said all this as a way of being nice to my mother again.

My mother nodded just slightly, looking toward the window. "Dunno," she said. A few minutes later, her eyes were closed.

Not until long after did I think that she might not have known the famous actress I mentioned. My brother said, many years later, that she had never been to a movie that he knew of. My brother has never been to a movie either. About Vicky, I don't know.

I saw the artist I had known in college a few years after I left the hospital, at an opening for another artist. It was a bad time in my marriage. Things had occurred that humiliated me; my husband had become very close to the woman who had brought my girls to the hospital and who had no children of her own. I had asked that she no longer come to our home, and he agreed. But I am quite sure we had an argument that night we went to the opening. And I remember that I did not change my top. It was a purple knit top, and I wore it with a skirt and I put on my husband's long blue coat at the last minute; my husband must have worn his leather jacket. I remember I was surprised to see the artist there. He seemed nervous to see me, and his eyes went over my purple knit top and the navy blue coat—they both fit me poorly, and the colors didn't go together; I did not see this until I got home and looked in the mirror and saw what he had seen. It didn't matter. My marriage mattered. But seeing the artist that night mattered enough that so many years later I can still picture the long blue coat and my garish purple top. He was still the only person who made me self-conscious about my clothes, and that—to me—was curious.

I have said before: It interests me how we find ways to feel superior to another person, another group of people. It happens everywhere, and all the time. Whatever we call it, I think it's the lowest part of who we are, this need to find someone else to put down.

The writer Sarah Payne, whom I had come across in the clothing store, was to speak on a panel at the New York Public Library. I read this in the newspaper a few months after I had seen her. I was surprised by it; she seldom appeared publicly, and I assumed she must be very private. When I mentioned this to someone who was said to know her peripherally, that person said, "She's not so private, New York just doesn't like her." And it reminded me of the man who had spoken of her as a good writer except for her tendency toward the compassionate. I went to see her on this panel; William did not go with me, he said he would rather stay at home with the children. It was in the summer, and there were not nearly as many people as I had thought there might be. The man who had said that about her—the compassion business—was sitting alone in the back row. The panel was about the idea of fiction: what it was, and that sort of thing. A character Sarah Payne had written about in one of her books had referred to a former American president as a "senile old man whose wife ruled the country with her astrology charts." Apparently Sarah Payne had received hate mail from people who said they had liked her book until they reached the part where this character referred to one of our presidents in this way. The moderator seemed surprised to hear this. "Really?" He was a librarian from the library. She said, "Really." "And do you answer such letters?" The librarian asked this while his fingers, with a certain precision, touched the bottom of his microphone. She said that she did not answer them. She said, and her face was not as sparkling as it had been when I came across her in the clothing store, "It's not my job to make readers know what's a narrative voice and not the private view of the author," and that alone made me glad I had come. The librarian seemed unable to understand. "What do you mean?" he kept saying, and she

97

only repeated what she had said before. He said, "What *is* your job as a writer of fiction?" And she said that her job as a writer of fiction was to report on the human condition, to tell us who we are and what we think and what we do.

A woman in the audience raised her hand and said, "But *do* you think that about the former president?"

Sarah Payne waited for a moment, then said, "Okay, I'll tell you this. If that woman I wrote about in a fictional way calls the man senile and old and says he has a wife who rules with her astrology charts, then I would say"—and she nodded her head tightly, and waited—"I, meaning me, Sarah Payne, citizen of this country, I would say, the woman I *made up* lets him off quite easily."

New York audiences can be tough, but they understood what she meant, and heads nodded and people whispered things to one another. I looked behind me at the man in the back row, and he appeared to be without emotion. At the end of the night I heard him say to a woman who'd come to speak to him, "She's always taken a stage well." He did not say it nicely, is how I felt. And I took the subway home alone; it was not a night I loved the city I have lived in for so long. But I could not have said exactly why. Almost, I could have said why. But not exactly why.

And so I began to record this story on that night. Parts of it.

I began to try.

The night in the hospital when I felt I had been unkind to my mother by saying that I did not think she ever cared what it was like to be famous, I couldn't fall asleep. I was agitated; I wanted to cry. When my own children cried I fell to pieces, I would kiss them and see what was wrong. Maybe I did it too much. And when I had had an argument with William, I sometimes cried, and I learned early that he was not a man who hated to hear a woman cry, as many men are, but that it would break whatever coldness was in him, and he would almost always hold me if I cried very hard and say, "It's okay, Button, we'll work it out." But with my mother I didn't dare cry. Both my parents loathed the act of crying, and it's difficult for a child who is crying to have to stop, knowing if she doesn't stop everything will be made worse. This is not an easy position for any child. And my mother—that night in the hospital room—was the mother I had had all my life, no matter how different she seemed with her urgent quiet voice, her softer face. What I mean is, I tried not to cry. In the dark I felt she was awake.

Then I felt her squeeze my foot through the sheet.

"Mommy," I said, bolting upright. "Mommy, please don't go!"

"I'm not going anywhere, Wizzle," she said. "I'm right here. You're going to be all right. You'll have a lot of stuff to face in your life, but people do. I've seen some of it in your case, I mean I've had some visions, but with you—"

I squeezed my eyes shut—*Don't you fucking cry you little idiot*—and I squeezed my leg so hard I almost could not believe how much it hurt. Then it was over. I turned onto my side. "With me what?" I said. I could say it calmly now.

"With you, I'm never sure how accurate these things are. They used to be accurate with you."

"Like when you knew I had Chrissie," I said.

"Yes. But I didn't—"

"Know her name." We spoke this together, and in the dark it felt to me that we smiled together too. My mother said, "Sleep, Wizzle, you need your sleep. And if you can't sleep, just rest."

In the morning the doctor came and swooshed the curtain about me, and when he saw the red bruise on my thigh he didn't touch it, but he stared at it, then he looked at me. He raised his eyebrows, and to my horror, tears slipped from the sides of my eyes. He nodded kindly, though it took him just a moment. He put his hand on my forehead, as though checking for a fever, and he left it there while the tears kept slipping from my eyes. He moved his thumb once, as though to brush away a tear. My God, he was kind. He was a kind, kind man. I gave a tiny smile to say thank you, a tiny grimace-smile to say that I was sorry.

He nodded and said, "You'll see those kids soon. We'll get you home with your husband. You're not going to die on my watch, I promise you." And then he made a fist and kissed it, and held it out toward me.

Sarah Payne was teaching a weeklong class in Arizona, and I was surprised when William offered to pay for me to go. This was a few months after I had seen her at the New York Public Library. I was not sure I wanted to be away from the children for that long, but William encouraged me. The class was called a "workshop," and I don't know why, but I have never liked that word: "workshop." I went because it was taught by Sarah Payne. When I saw her in the classroom I gave a bright smile, thinking she would remember me from our meeting in the clothing store. But she only nodded back, and it took me some moments to realize she didn't recognize me. Perhaps it is true that we wish for some tiny acknowledgment from someone famous, that they see us.

Our class met in an old building on the top of a hill, and it was warm and the windows were open, and I watched as Sarah Payne became exhausted almost immediately. I saw it in her face. By the end of one hour her face looked like it had fallen the way white clay loses its shape when it's not cold enough, that is the image, that her face had dropped into a strange shape from fatigue, and at the end of three hours it seemed even more so, as though her white clay face was almost trembling. It took everything out of her to teach that class, is what I am saying. Her face was just ravaged with fatigue. Every day she would start with a little of the sparkle, and within minutes the fatigue set in. I don't think I have seen before or since a face that showed its exhaustion so clearly.

There was a man in the class who had recently lost his wife to cancer, and Sarah was nice to him, I saw this. We all, I felt, saw this. We saw that this man fell in love with a student in the class who was a friend of Sarah's. It was fine. The friend did not fall back in love with him, but she treated him decently, there was something decent in the way this woman and Sarah treated this man who was in pain from the death of his wife. There was also a woman who taught English. There was a Canadian man who had pink cheeks and a very pleasant way about him; the class teased him about being so Canadian, and he took it well. There was another woman who was a psychoanalyst from California.

And I want to report here what happened one day, which is that through the open window a cat suddenly jumped into the room, right onto the large table. The cat was huge, and long; in my memory he may as well have been a small tiger. I jumped up with terrible fear, and Sarah Payne jumped up as well; terribly she jumped, she had been that frightened. And then the cat ran out through the door of the classroom. The psychoanalyst woman from California, who usually said very little, said that day to Sarah Payne, in a voice that was—to my ears—almost snide, "How long have you suffered from post-traumatic stress?"

And what I remember is the look on Sarah's face. She hated this woman for saying that. She hated her. There was a silence long enough that people saw this on Sarah's face, this is how I think of it anyway. Then the man who had lost his wife said, "Well, hey, that was a really big cat."

After that, Sarah talked a lot to the class about judging people, and about coming to the page without judgment.

We were promised a private conference in this workshop situation, and I am sure Sarah must have been very tired with the private conferences. People tend to go to these workshops because they want to be discovered and get published. For the workshop I had brought parts of the novel I was writing, but when I had my conference with Sarah I took instead sketches of scenes of my mother coming to visit me in the hospital, things I had started to write after I had seen Sarah at the library; I had slipped a copy of the pages to her the day before, in her mailbox. I remember mostly that she spoke to me as though I had known her a long time, even though she never mentioned our having met at the clothing store. "I'm sorry I'm so tired," she said. "Jesus, I'm almost dizzy." She leaned forward, touching my knee lightly before she sat back. "Honestly," she said softly, "with that last person I thought I was going to be sick. Like really throw-up sick, I'm just not cut out for this." Then she said, "Listen to me, and listen to me carefully. What you are writing, what you want to write," and she leaned forward again and tapped with her finger the piece I had given her, "this is very good and it will be published. Now listen. People will go after you for combining poverty and abuse. *Such* a stupid word, 'abuse,' such a conventional and stupid word, but people will say there's poverty without abuse, and you will never say anything. Never ever defend your work. This is a story about love, you know that. This is a story of a man who has been tortured every day of his life for things he did in the war. This is the story of a wife who stayed with him, because most wives did in that generation, and she comes to her daughter's hospital room and talks compulsively about everyone's marriage going bad, she doesn't even know it, doesn't even know that's what she's doing. This is a story about a mother who loves her daughter. Imperfectly. Because we *all* love imperfectly. But if you find yourself protecting anyone as you write this piece, remember this: You're not doing it right." She sat back then, and wrote down titles of books I should read, most of them classics, and when she stood and I stood to leave, she suddenly said, "Wait," and then she hugged me, and made a kissing sound to her fingers, which she held by her lips, and it made me think of the kind doctor.

I said, "I was sorry that woman in class asked about PTSD. I jumped too."

Sarah said, "I know you did, I saw that. And anyone who uses their training to put someone down that way—well, that person is just a big old piece of crap." She winked at me, her face exhausted, and turned to go.

I have never seen her since.

"Say," my mother said. This was the fourth day my mother had been sitting at the foot of my bed. "You remember that Marilyn girl—what was her name, Marilyn Mathews, I don't know what her name was. Marilyn Somebody. Do you remember her?"

"I remember her. Yeah," I said. "Sure."

"What was her name?" my mother asked.

"Marilyn Somebody," I said.

"She married Charlie Macauley. Do you remember him? Sure you do. You don't? He was from Carlisle, and—well, I guess he was more your brother's age. They didn't go out in high school, he and Marilyn. But they got married, they both went to college—in Wisconsin I think, at Madison—and—"

I said, "Charlie Macauley. Wait. He was tall. They were in high school when I was still in junior high. Marilyn went to our church and she helped her mother serve the food for Thanksgiving dinners."

"Oh, of course. That's right." My mother nodded. "You're right. Marilyn was a very nice person. And I told you that already—that she was more your brother's age."

I suddenly had a clear memory of Marilyn smiling at me one day when she passed me in the empty hall after school, and it was a nice smile, like she was sorry for me, but I felt she did not want her smile to seem condescending. That was why I always remembered her.

"*Why* would you remember her?" my mother said to me. "If she was older like that. Because of the Thanksgiving dinners?"

"Why would *you* remember her?" I said to my mother. "What happened to her? And why would you know?"

"Oh." My mother let out a great sigh and shook her head. "A woman came into the library the other day— I go to the library in Hanston some days now—and this woman looked like her, like Marilyn. I said, 'You look like someone I knew, who was about the age of my kids.' And she didn't answer, and that—that makes me very angry, you know."

I did know. I had lived my life with that feeling. That people did not want to acknowledge us, be friends with us. "Oh, Mom," I said tiredly. "Screw 'em."

"*Screw* them?"

"You know what I mean."

"I see you've learned lots living in the big city."

I smiled at the ceiling. I didn't know a person in the world who would have believed this conversation, yet it was as true as any can be. "Mom, I didn't have to move to the big city to learn to say 'screw.'"

There was a silence, as though my mother was considering this. Then she said, "No, you probably only had to walk to the Pedersons' barn and hear their hired hands."

"The hired hands said a lot more than the word 'screw,'" I told her.

"I imagine they did," my mother said.

And this is when—recording this—I think once more, Why did I not just ask her then? Why did I not just say, Mom, I learned all the words I needed to right in that *fucking* garage we called home? I suspect I said nothing because I was doing what I have done most of my life, which is to cover for the mistakes of others when they don't know they have embarrassed themselves. I do this, I think, because it could be me a great deal of the time. I know faintly, even now, that I have embarrassed myself, and it always comes back to the feeling of childhood, that huge pieces of knowledge about the world were missing that can never be replaced. But still— I do it for others, even as I sense that others do it for me. And I can only think I did it for my mother that day. Who else would not have sat up and said, Mom, do you not remember?

I have asked experts. Kind ones, like the doctor who was kind; not unkind people, like the woman who spoke so meanly to Sarah Payne when she jumped at the cat. Their answers have been thoughtful, and almost always the same: I don't know what your mother remembered. I like these experts because they seem decent, and because I feel I know a true sentence when I hear one now. They do not know what my mother remembered.

I don't know what my mother remembered either.

"But it did get me thinking about Marilyn," my mother continued in her breathy voice, "and so I asked later in the week when I saw that so-and-so person from the—oh, you know, Wizzle, the place—"

"Chatwin's Cake Shoppe."

"That place," my mother said. "Yes, the woman who still works there—she knows everything."

"Evelyn."

"Evelyn. So I sat down and had a piece of cake and a cup of coffee and I said to her, 'You know, I thought I saw Marilyn what's-her-name the other day,' and this Evelyn, I always liked her—"

"I loved her," I said. I did not say I loved her because she was good to my cousin Abel, good to me, that she never said a word when she saw us going through the dumpster. And my mother did not ask why I loved her.

My mother said, "Well, she stopped wiping the counter and she said to me, 'Poor Marilyn married that Charlie Macauley from Carlisle, I think they still live nearby now, but she married him back when they were in college, and he was a smart fellow. So of course they take the smart ones right away.'"

"Who takes them?" I asked.

"Why, our dirty rotten government, of course," my mother answered.

I said nothing, just looked up at the ceiling. It has been my experience throughout life that the people who have been given the most by our government—education, food, rent subsidies—are the ones who are most apt to find fault with the whole idea of government. I understand this in a way.

"What did they take Marilyn's smart husband for?" I asked.

"Well, they made him an officer, of course. During those Vietnam years. And I guess he had to do some terrible stuff, and from what Evelyn was telling me, he's never been the same. So early in their marriage this happened, very sad. Very, very sad," my mother said.

I waited quite a while, quite a while I waited, lying there with my heart thumping, I can remember even now the thumping, the banging of my heart, and I thought of what I had—to myself—always called the *Thing*, the most horrifying part of my childhood. I was very frightened lying there, I was frightened that my mother would mention it after all these years, after never mentioning it ever, and I finally said, "But what does he do—as a result of this experience? Is he mean to Marilyn?"

"I don't know," my mother said. Her voice seemed suddenly tired. "I don't know what it is he does. Maybe there's help these days. At least there's a name. It's not like they were the first people to be trauma—whatever the word is—by a war."

In my memory of this, I was the one to get us away

as fast as we could now, as fast as we could, from where my mother may—or may not—have known she was headed.

"I hate to think of anyone being mean to Marilyn," I said, then I added that the doctor hadn't yet come in to see me.

"It's Saturday," my mother said.

"He'll come anyway. He always does."

"He won't work on a Saturday," my mother said. "He told you yesterday to have a good weekend. To me that doesn't sound like he works on a Saturday."

Then I became afraid. I became afraid that she was right. "Oh, Mommy," I said, "I'm so tired. I want to get better."

"You'll get better," she said. "I've seen it clearly. You'll get better, and you'll have some problems in your life. But what matters is, you'll get better."

"Are you sure?"

"I am sure."

"What problems?" I asked this in a way that tried to sound joking, as though what did I care about a few problems?

"Problems." My mother was quiet for a while. "Like most people have, or some people. Marriage problems. Your kids will be all right."

115

"How do you know?"

"How do I know? I don't know how I know. I've never known how I know."

"I know," I said.

"You rest, Lucy."

It was still the beginning of June, and the days were very long. It was not until the lights were just starting to show in the dusk through the window that gave us the magnificent view of the city that I heard the voice at my door. "Girls," he said.

We had been living in the West Village a few years when I attended my first Gay Pride Parade, and living in the Village made the parade a big deal. This was natural. There had been the history of Stonewall, and then the awful business of AIDS, and many people came to line the streets and be supportive and also to celebrate and mourn those who had died. I held Chrissie's hand, and William held Becka on his hip. We stood and watched as men walked by in purple high heels and wigs and some in dresses, then there were mothers who marched by, and all the kinds of things you see at such an event in New York.

William turned to me and said, "Lucy, Jesus Christ,

come *on*," because of what he saw in my face, and I shook my head and turned to go home, and he came with me and said, "Oh, Button. I remember now."

He was the only person I had told.

Perhaps my brother was a freshman in high school. He may have been a year older, he may have been a year younger. But we still lived in the garage, so I would have been about ten. Because my mother took in sewing, she kept various pairs of high heels in her basket in the corner of the garage. That basket might have been like another woman's closet. In it were also brassieres and girdles and a garter belt. I think that those were for women who needed some alteration done and had not arrived with the right underclothes; even when it was normal for all women to wear these things, my mother did not bother to wear them, unless she had a customer coming over.

Vicky came shrieking toward the schoolyard to find me that day, I don't even know if it was a school day or why she wasn't with me, I only remember her shriek and the gathering of people and the laughter. My father was driving our truck along the main street in town and he was screaming at my brother, who was walking down the street in a pair of big high heels I recognized from the basket, and a bra over his T-shirt, and a string of fake pearls, and his face was streaming with tears. My father drove alongside him in our truck screaming that he was a fucking faggot and the world should know. I could not believe what I saw, and I took Vicky's hand, though I was the youngest, and I walked her all the way home. My mother was there and said that our brother had been found wearing her clothes, and it was disgusting and my father was teaching him a lesson and Vicky should stop her noise, and so I took Vicky away in the fields until it was dark and we became more afraid of the dark than of our home. I still am not sure it's a true memory, except I do know it, I think. I mean: It is true. Ask anyone who knew us.

That day of the parade in the Village, I think—but I'm not sure—that William and I had a fight. Because I remember him saying, "Button, you just don't get it, do you?" He meant I did not understand that I could be loved, was lovable. Very often he said that when we had a fight. He was the only man to call me "Button." But he was not the last to say the other: You just don't get it, do you?

———

Sarah Payne, the day she told us to go to the page without judgment, reminded us that we never knew, and never would know, what it would be like to understand another person fully. It seems a simple thought, but as I get older I see more and more that she had to tell us that. We think, always we think, What is it about someone that makes us despise that person, that makes us feel superior? I will say that that night—I remember this part more than what I just described—my father lay next to my brother in the dark and held him as though he was a baby, he rocked him on his lap and I could not tell one's tears and murmurs from the other's.

"Elvis," my mother said. It was nighttime; the room was dark except for the lights of the city through the window.

"Elvis Presley?"

"Is there another Elvis you know of?" my mother asked.

"No. You said 'Elvis.'" I waited. I said, "Why did you say 'Elvis,' Mom?"

"He was famous."

"He was. He was so famous, he died from it."

"He died from drugs, Lucy."

"But that would be the loneliness thing, Mom. From

being so famous. Think about it: He couldn't go anywhere."

For a long time my mother said nothing. I had the feeling she was really thinking about this. She said, "I liked his early stuff. Your father thought he was the Devil himself, the foolish things he wore in the end, but if you just heard his voice, Lucy—"

"Mom. I've *heard* his voice. I didn't know you knew anything about Elvis. Mom, when did you listen to Elvis?"

Again there was a long silence, and then my mother said, "Eh—he was just a Tupelo boy. A poor boy from Tupelo, Mississippi, who loved his mama. He appeals to cheap people. That's who likes him, cheapies." She waited, and then she said, her voice for the first time, really, becoming the voice from my childhood, "Your father was right. He's just a big old piece of trash."

Trash.

"He's a dead piece of trash," I said.

"Well, sure. Drugs."

I said, finally, "We were trash. That's exactly what we were."

In the voice from my childhood, my mother said, "Lucy Damn-dog Barton. I didn't fly across the country to have you tell me that we are trash. My ancestors and your father's ancestors, we were some of the first people in this country, Lucy Barton. I did *not* fly across the country to have you tell me that we're trash. They were good decent people. They came ashore at Province-town, Massachusetts, and they were fishermen and they were *settlers*. We settled this country, and the good brave ones later moved to the Midwest, and that's who we are, that's who *you* are. And don't you ever forget it."

It took me a few moments before I said, "I won't." And then I said, "No, I'm sorry, Mom. I am."

She was silent. I felt I could feel her fury, and I sort of felt, too, that her having said this would keep me in the hospital longer; I mean, I felt it in my body. I wanted to say, *Go home*. Go home and tell people how we weren't trash, tell people how your ancestors came here and murdered all the Indians, Mom! Go home and tell them all.

Maybe I didn't want to tell her that. Maybe that's just what I think now as I write this.

A poor boy from Tupelo who loved his mama. A poor girl from Amgash who loved her mama too.

I have used the word "trash," as my mother did that day in the hospital as she spoke of Elvis Presley. I used it with a good friend I made not long after I left the hospital—she is the best woman friend I have made in my life—and she told me, after I met her, after my mother came to see me in the hospital, that she and her mother would fight and they hit each other, and I said to her: "That's so trashy."

And she, my friend, said, "Well, we were trash."

In my memory her voice was defensive and angry; why would it not have been? I've never told her how I felt, that it was so wrong of me to have said it. My friend is older than I am, she knows more than I do, and

perhaps she knows—and she was raised a Congrega-
tionalist too—that we won't speak of it. Perhaps she
forgot. I don't think she has.

This too:

Right after I found out about my college admission,
I showed my high school English teacher a story I had
written. I can remember very little of it, but I remember
this: He had circled the word "cheap." The sentence
was something like "The woman wore a cheap dress."
Don't use that word, he said, it is not nice and it is not
accurate. I don't know if he said that exactly—but he
had circled the word and gently told me something
about it that was not nice or good, and I have remembered that always.

"Say, Wizzle," my mother said.

It was early morning. Cookie had been in, taken my temperature, asked if I wanted some juice. I said I would try the juice, and she left. In spite of my anger, I had slept. But my mother looked very tired. She seemed no longer angry, just tired, and more like the person she had been since she'd arrived to see me at the hospital. "Do you remember me talking about Mississippi Mary?"

"No. Yes. Wait. Was she Mary Mumford with all those Mumford girls?"

"Oh yes, you're right! She married that Mumford fellow. Yes, all those girls. Evelyn in Chatwin's Cake

Shoppe used to talk about her, they were related some-how. Evelyn's husband was a cousin, I don't remember. But 'Mississippi Mary,' Evelyn called her. Poor as a church mouse. I got to thinking of her after we spoke of Elvis. She was from Tupelo too. But her father moved the family to Illinois—Carlisle—and that's where she grew up. I don't know why they moved to Illinois, but her father worked at the gas station there. Not a South-ern accent on her. Poor Mary. But she was cute as the dickens, and she was the head cheerleader, and she mar-ried the captain of the football team, the Mumford boy, and *he* had money."

My mother's voice was rushed again, compressed.

"Mom—"

She waved a hand at me. "Listen, Wizzle, if you want a good story. *Listen*. Write *this* one up. So, Evelyn told me when I was in there talking about—"

"Marilyn Somebody." We said this together, and my mother paused to smile; oh, I loved her, my mother!

"Listen. So Mississippi Mary married this rich fel-low and had, oh, I don't know, five or six girls, I think they were all girls, and she was a pleasant person and they lived on a big place where her husband ran his business, I don't know what business it was— And her husband would take trips for his business, and it turned out that for thirteen years he was having an affair with his secretary, and the secretary was a fat thing, such a fat, *fat* thing, and Mary finally found out and she had a heart attack."

"Did she die?"

"Nope. No, don't think so." My mother sat back, she looked exhausted.

"Mom. That's sad."

"Of course it's sad!"

We were silent for a while. Then my mother said, "I only remembered her because she—well, all of this according to her cousin Evelyn at Chatwin's—she *loved* Elvis, born in that same dump he came from."

"Mom."

"What, Lucy?" She turned and looked at me quickly.

I said, "I'm glad you're here."

My mother nodded and looked out the window again. "I've thought how strange it must be. Both Elvis and Mississippi Mary went from being so poor to being very wealthy—and it didn't seem to have done either of them a damn bit of good."

"No, of course not," I said.

I have gone to places in this city where the very wealthy go. One place is a doctor's office. Women, and a few men, sit in the waiting room for the doctor who will make them look not old or worried or like their mother. A few years ago I went there to not look like my mother. The doctor said that almost everyone came in the first time and said they looked like their mother and didn't want to. I had seen my father in my face too, and she, the doctor, said, yes, she could help with that as well. Usually it was the mother—or the father—that people didn't want to look like, often both, she said, but mostly it was the mother. She put tiny needles into the wrinkles by my mouth. You are beautiful now, she said. You look like yourself. Come back in three days and let me see.

Three days later in the waiting room was a woman who was terribly old, and she had a brace on her back, which was bent almost in half. She smiled from a face that had been made to look years younger. I thought she was brave. Beside me sat a young boy, perhaps in middle school, and his older sister. They may have been waiting for their mother—I don't know who they were waiting for. But they were wealthy. You get to have a feel for this, even if I hadn't been in this office of this doctor. I watched the young boy and his sister. They spoke of calling Pips, and the girl said, I can only call national numbers, I can't call international on this phone. The boy was nice about that; he suggested a way to email Pips and have Pips call them. Then I watched this boy watch the very old lady, he watched her with interest, and yet because she was so bent over, she was for him of course a different species. This is how old she looked to him, I could see this; I felt I could see this. I loved the boy and his sister. They looked healthy and beautiful and good. And the very old lady took her leave, slowly. She had a bright pink ribbon tied to her cane.

The boy got up suddenly and opened the door for her.

This is some city. But I have already said that.

That night in the hospital, the last night my mother stayed with me—she had been there five days—I thought about my brother. I remembered then how I had come across a group of boys in the field by the school, I must have been about six years old, and I saw that there was fighting, that a kid was being hit by a group of boys. The boy being hit was my brother. His face looked like he was paralyzed with fear, and in fact he did not seem to move, he was crouched while these boys hit him. I saw this only briefly, because I turned and ran away. I thought too—that night in the hospital—how my brother had not had to go to the war in Vietnam be-cause his number in the lottery was a good one. Before he found out, I remember hearing my parents speaking at night, and I heard my father say: The army will kill him, we can't let it happen, the army will be terrible for him. And it was soon after that, we found out that my brother's number was a good one. But my father loved him! I saw this that night.

And then I remembered this: There was a Labor Day when my father took me, alone—I don't know why I was alone with him; I mean, I don't know where my brother and sister were—to Moline, about forty miles away. Perhaps he had business there, though it is hard to imagine what possible type of business he had anywhere, let alone in Moline, but I do remember being there with him for the Black Hawk Festival, and we watched the dancing of the Indians. The Indian women stood in a circle around the men, and the women only took little steps while the men danced with much commotion. My father seemed keenly interested in watching the dancing and the festivities. There were candied apples for sale, and I wanted one desperately. I had never had a candied apple. My father bought one for me. It was an astonishing thing for him to have done that. And I remember that I couldn't eat the apple, I couldn't get my small teeth into the red crust, and I felt desolation, and he took it from me and he ate it, but his brow became furrowed, and I felt that I had caused him worry. I don't remember watching the dancers after that, I remember watching only my father's face, so high above me, and I saw his lips become reddish with the candied apple that he ate because he had to. In my memory I love him for this, since he did not yell at me, or make me feel bad for not being able to eat the apple, but took it from me, and ate it himself, even with no pleasure.

And I remembered this: that he was interested in what he was watching. He had an *interest* in it. What did he think of those Indians who were dancing?

I said suddenly, as the lights started to come on throughout the city, "Mommy, do you love me?"

My mother shook her head, looked out at the lights. "Wizzle, stop."

"Come on, Mom, tell me." I began to laugh, and she began to laugh too.

"Wizzle, for heaven's sake."

I sat up and, like a child, clapped my hands. "Mom! Do you love me, do you love me, do you love me?"

She flicked her hand at me, still looking out the window. "Silly girl," she said, and shook her head. "You silly, silly girl."

I lay back down and closed my eyes. I said, "Mom, my eyes are closed."

"Lucy, you stop it now." I heard the mirth in her voice.

"Come on, Mom. My eyes are closed."

There was a silence for a while. I was happy. "Mom?" I said.

"When your eyes are closed," she said.

"You love me when my eyes are closed?"

"When your eyes are closed," she said. And we stopped the game, but I was so happy—

Sarah Payne said, If there is a weakness in your story, address it head-on, take it in your teeth and address it, before the reader really knows. This is where you will get your authority, she said, during one of those classes when her face was filled with fatigue from teaching. I feel that people may not understand that my mother could never say the words I love you. I feel that people may not understand: It was all right.

It was the next day in the hospital—Monday—when Cookie said I needed just one more X-ray; it would be simple, she said, they'd be up to get me soon. Within an hour I was back in the room. My mother wiggled her fingers at me, and I wiggled mine back once I returned to my bed. "Piece of cake," I said to her. And she said, "You're a brave girl, Wizzle-dee." She looked out the window, and I looked out the window too.

We must have spoken more, I'm sure we did. But then my doctor came in hurriedly and said, "We might have to take you to surgery. You may have a blockage, I don't like what I see."

"I *can't*," I said, sitting up. "I'll die if I have surgery. Look how skinny I've gotten!"

My doctor said, "Except for being sick, you're healthy and you're young."

My mother stood up. "It's time for me to go home," she said.

"Mommy, no, you can't!" I cried.

"Yes. I've been here long enough, and it's time I go home."

My doctor had no response to my mother's remark. I remember only his determination to get me to the next test to see if I needed surgery. And while I would stay in the hospital for almost five weeks more, he never asked me about my mother, if I missed her, never said that it must have been nice to have her there, not one thing about her did he say. And so I never told this kind doctor how I missed her terribly, that her coming was— well, I couldn't have said what it was. And I didn't say anything about it at all.

So my mother left that day. She was frightened about how she would find a cab. I asked one of the nurses to help her, but I knew that once she reached First Avenue, no nurse would be able to help her. Already two male orderlies had brought the gurney into my room, and the bed rail was taken down. I told my mother how to raise her arm, how to say "La Guardia" as though she said it often. But I could see that she was terrified, and I was terrified too. I have no idea if she kissed me goodbye, but I cannot think she would have. I have no memory of my mother ever kissing me. She may have kissed me though; I may be wrong.

I have said that at the time I am writing about, the AIDS disease was a terrible thing. It's still a terrible thing, but people are used to it now. Being used to it is not good. But when I was in the hospital, the disease was new and no one yet understood how to keep it in abeyance, and so on the door of a hospital room in which a person had this illness would be a yellow sticker, I can remember them still. Yellow stickers with black lines. When I later went to Germany with William I thought of the yellow stickers in the hospital. They did not say ACHTUNG! But they were like that. And I thought of the yellow stars the Nazis made the Jews wear.

My mother had left so quickly, and I had been taken

away on a gurney so quickly, that when I was suddenly brought out of the big elevator and parked by a wall in a hallway on a different floor, it was surprising to me that I was left there for so long. But what happened is this: I was left in a place where I could see across the hall to a room with that terrible yellow sticker on the partly opened door, and I saw a man with dark eyes and dark hair in the bed, and he was, it seemed to me, staring at me every second. I felt terrible that he was dying, and I knew that dying that way was a terrible death. I was afraid of dying, but I did not have his illness, and he had to know that—they would not have left a patient in the hallway like they left me there, had I had that illness. I felt in this man's gaze that he was begging me for something. I tried to look away, to give him privacy, but each time I glanced at him again he was still staring at me. There are times still I think of those dark eyes in the face of the man lying on that bed, peering at me with what in my memory I think of as despair, begging. I have since then—it's natural as we get older—been with people as they died, and I've come to recognize the eyes that burn, the very last of the body's light to go out. In a way that man helped me that day. His eyes said: I will not look away. And I was afraid of him, of death, of my mother leaving me. But his eyes never looked away.

I did not have more surgery. Again my doctor said that he was sorry to have frightened me, but I only shook my head to let him know that I knew he loved me in his doctor-way and that he had only been trying to keep me alive. Every Friday he said what my mother had heard him say, "Have a good weekend, then, if you can." And every Saturday and every Sunday he would show up, saying he had another patient to check on and he was stopping by, therefore, to check on me as well. He only did not come on Father's Day. I was so jealous of his children! Father's Day! I have never met his children, of course. I heard that his son became a doctor, and later—a few years later, when I saw him in his office and it came up in conversation how I was worried about one of my girls not having many friends—he gave me good advice, citing one of his own girls, saying she now had more friends than his other children, and this has turned out to be true for the daughter I was worried about too. When I had trouble in my marriage—I mentioned it to him briefly—this kind doctor was frightened for me. I do remember I saw that, and that he had no advice to give me. But for those nine weeks that spring and summer so long ago now—for nine weeks minus one day, Father's Day—this man, this lovely doctor father-man, saw me every day, sometimes twice a day. When I left and the bills came in, he charged me for five hospital visits. I want to record that too.

I was worried about my mother. She had not called to tell me she had made it home, and I could only make local calls on the phone by my bed. Or I could make collect calls, which would mean that whoever answered in my childhood home would be asked if they would accept the charges; that is how it was done. An operator would say: "Will you accept the charges of Lucy Barton?" One time only had I called them like this, it was when I was pregnant with my second child and I had had some sort of altercation with William, I have no memory about what. But I missed my mother, I missed my father, I suddenly missed the stark tree in the corn-field of my youth, I missed this all so deeply and terribly that I pushed the stroller with little Chrissie in it to a telephone booth by Washington Square Park and I called my parents' home. My mother answered, and the operator said that Lucy Barton was on the line calling from New York, would my mother accept the charges?, and my mother said, "No. You tell that girl she has money now to spend, and she can spend it on her own." I hung up before the operator had to repeat this to me. And so that night in the hospital I did not call my parents to see if my mother had gotten home. But William called them from our apartment in the Village, because I asked him to. And he said yes, she had arrived safely back at her home.

"Did she say anything else?" I asked. I was terribly sad. I was as sad, really, as a sad child, and children can be very sad.

"Oh, Button," my husband said. "Button. No."

The next week, my friend Molla came to visit. She said, sitting right next to the head of the bed, so close, it seemed, Nice to have had your mother here, and I said yes, and she told me that she hated her mother terrifically, and told me the whole story again as though she had not told it to me before, how much she hated her mother, and when she'd had her babies she had to see a psychiatrist because she was saddened by everything her mother had not given her. Molla said all this to me that day, and recording this now I think of something Sarah Payne had said at the writing class in Arizona. "You will have only one story," she had said.

"You'll write your one story many ways. Don't ever worry about story. You have only one."

I smiled at Molla as she talked, I was very glad to see her. I asked her finally about my own children, did they seem terribly distressed I was not around? She said she thought that Chrissie seemed more able to understand, she was the older one, so that would be natural; Chrissie had a long talk on the stoop with Molla, and Molla had listened as Chrissie told her Mommy was sick but getting better. "You did tell her I was getting better, didn't you?" I said, trying to sit up. And Molla said she had. I loved Molla for this, for her concern about my darling Chrissie. I asked her about Jeremy, how was he?

And she said she hadn't seen him, he must be away. I told her that was what my husband had said too.

Molla chatted then about other mothers she knew from the park, one was moving to the suburbs, another was moving uptown.

When she left, I was exhausted. But I had been glad to see her. I thanked her for coming. She said, Of course, and she bent down and kissed my head.

My husband came to visit. It may have been a week-end day, I can only think it must have been. He seemed very tired and he did not say much. He was a big man, but he lay down next to me on my skinny bed and ran his hand through his blond hair. He turned on the tele-vision that hung above the bed. He was paying for me to have it, but because I didn't have one growing up, I think I've never quite understood television. And in the hos-pital I seldom put it on, because I associated it with people being sick during the day. Whenever I was told to walk the halls for exercise, pushing my little apparatus of IV bags, I saw that most patients just stared at their televisions, and it made me feel very sad. But my husband turned it on, and he lay next to me on the bed. I wanted to talk, but he was tired. We lay quietly that way.

My doctor seemed surprised to see him. Perhaps he was not at all surprised, but I thought he seemed that way. And he said something about how nice it was, that we could be together like this, and I remember a twing or twang in my head, I didn't know why. No one knows why until later.

I know that my husband came more than that one day to visit me. But it is that day I remember, and so I write it down. This is not the story of my marriage. I cannot tell that story: I cannot take hold of, or lay out for anyone, the many swamps and grasses and pockets of fresh air and dank air that have gone over us. But I can tell you this: My mother was right; I had trouble in my marriage. And when my girls were nineteen and twenty years old, I left their father, and we have both remarried. There are days when I feel I love him more than I did when I was married to him, but that is an easy thing to think—we are free of each other, and yet not, and never will be. And there are days when I have such a clear image of him sitting at his desk in his study while the girls played in their room that I almost cry out: *We were a family!* I think of cellphones now, how quickly we are in touch. I remember when the girls were young I said to William, I wish there was something we could each wear on our wrists, like a phone, and then we could talk to each other and know where the other was all the time.

But that day that he came to see me in the hospital, when we barely spoke, it might have been when he had found out his father had left him no small amount of money in a Swiss bank account. His grandfather had profited on the war, and had put no small amount of money into a Swiss bank account, and now that William had turned thirty-five, the money was suddenly his. I learned about this later, when I came home. But it must have made William feel strange to think what the money was and what it meant, and he was never a person who could speak easily of his feelings, and so he lay on the bed with me, I who had—as we joked over the years, or perhaps only I joked—I, who had "come from nothing."

When I first met my mother-in-law she was a great surprise to me. Her house seemed enormous and well-appointed, but over the years I came to see that it was not so, it was just a nice house, a nice middle-class house. Because she had been a farmer's wife in Maine, and I thought of Maine as smaller in their farms than the Midwestern ones I knew, I had pictured her to look like some of the hired hands' wives, but she didn't look like that, she was a pleasing-looking woman who looked—she was fifty-five—no older than she was, and who moved through her lovely house with ease, a woman who had been married to a civil engineer. The first time I met her she said, "Lucy, let's take you shopping and buy you some clothes." I did not take offense, I didn't take anything but some surprise—no one had ever said such a thing to me in my life. And I went shopping with her, and she bought me some clothes.

At our small wedding reception she said to a friend of hers, "This is Lucy." She added, almost playfully, "Lucy comes from nothing." I took no offense, and really, I take none now. But I think: No one in this world comes from nothing.

Yet there was this: After I left the hospital I had recurring dreams that I, and my babies, were to be killed by the Nazis. Even now, so many years later, I can remember the dreams. In what looked like a locker room, I had my two little girls with me; they were both very young.

In the dream I understood—we all understood, for there were others in this locker room—that we were to be taken and killed by the Nazis. At first we thought that this room was a gas chamber, but we came to understand that instead the Nazis would come and take us to another room and that would be the gas chamber. I sang to my babies, and held them, and they were not afraid. I kept them off in a corner, away from the other people. And the situation was this: I accepted my death but did not want my children to be afraid. I was terribly scared they would be taken from me, perhaps they would be adopted by the Germans, for they looked like the little Aryan children they were. I could not bear to think of them mistreated, and there was some sense—a knowledge—in the dream that they would be mistreated. It was the most terrifying dream. It never went beyond that. I don't know how long I had this dream. But I had it as I lived in New York, with some affluence and as my children were growing and healthy. And I never told my husband that I had this dream.

I wrote my mother a letter. I said I loved her, and I thanked her for coming to see me in the hospital. I said I would never forget that she did that. She wrote back to me on a card that showed the Chrysler Building at night. Where she got that card in Amgash, Illinois, I cannot imagine, but she sent it to me and said *I will never forget either.* She signed it *M*. I put the card on my table near the telephone by my bed and looked at it often. I would pick it up and hold it, looking at her handwriting, no longer familiar to me. I still have the card with the Chrysler Building at night that she sent to me.

When I was able to leave the hospital, my shoes did

not fit. I had not thought that losing weight meant losing it everywhere, but it did—of course—and my shoes were too big on my feet. I packed the card in the bottom of the plastic bag they gave me to put my things in. My husband and I took a taxi home, and I remember that outside the hospital the world seemed very bright—frighteningly bright—and I did feel frightened by that. My children wanted to sleep with me on my first night home, and William said no, but they lay on the bed with me, my two girls. Dear God, I was happy to see my children, they had grown so. Becka had a terrible haircut; she had got gum in her hair, and the family friend who had no children of her own, who had brought them to me in the hospital, had cut her hair for her.

Jeremy.

I didn't know he was gay. I didn't know he was sick. No, said my husband, he never looked sick the way so many do. And now he was gone—he had died—while I was away. I wept steadily, a quiet weeping. On the front stoop I sat while Becka patted my head, Chrissie sometimes sat down next to me, putting her small arms around me, before the girls danced up and down the stairs again. Molla came by and said, Oh dear, you've heard about Jeremy. She said it was very bad, a terrible thing to happen to men. And women, she added. She sat with me while I wept.

I have thought so often—*so often*—about the man in the hospital with the yellow sticker on the door the day my mother left and I was parked in the hallway outside his room. How he looked at me with the dark of his burning eyes, begging, and with despair. Not letting me look away. It could have been Jeremy. Many times I have thought: I will look it up, it must be in the public records, the day he died and where he died. But I have never looked it up.

It was summer when I came home, and I wore sleeveless dresses, and I didn't realize I was so skinny. But I saw people look at me with fear when I went down the street to get food for the children. I was furious that they looked at me with fear. It was not unlike how children on our school bus would look at me if they thought I might sit next to them.

The gaunt and bony men continued to walk by.

When I was a child, our family went to the Congregational church. We were outcasts there as much as anywhere; even the Sunday school teacher ignored us. Once I came late to the class, the chairs were all taken. The teacher said, "Just sit on the floor, Lucy." Thanksgivings we went to the activities room in the church and we were given a Thanksgiving dinner. People were nicer to us on that day. Marilyn, whom my mother mentioned in the hospital, was there with her own mother sometimes, and she would serve us the string beans and the gravy and put the rolls on the table with their small plastic-covered butter pads. I think people even sat at a table with us, I don't remember that we were scorned at those Thanksgiving meals. For many years William and I went to shelters in New York on Thanksgiving and served food we had brought. It never felt to me that I was giving back. It felt like the turkey or the ham we brought with us seemed suddenly very small in the shelters—even if they were not vast—that we went to. In New York, they were not Congregationalists we fed. They were often people of color and they were sometimes people with mental illness, and William said one year, "I can't do this anymore," and I said that was okay, and I stopped doing it too.

But people who are cold! This I cannot stand! I read an article in the newspaper about an elderly couple in the Bronx who could not pay their heating bills, and they sat in their kitchen with the oven on. Every year I have given money so that people won't be cold. William gives money too. But to record that I give money for people to be warm is something that makes me feel uncomfortable. My mother would say, Stop your foolish bragging, Lucy Damn-dog Barton—

The kind doctor said it might take a long while for me
to gain my weight back, and I remember that he was
right, though I don't remember how long the long was.
I went to him for checkups, at first every two weeks,
then once a month. I tried to look nice; I remember I
would try on different outfits and look in the mirror to
see what he would see. In his office he had people in his
waiting room, people in his examining rooms, then in
his own office, a sort of conveyor belt of many kinds of
human material. I thought of how many people's be-
hinds he had seen, how different they all must be. I always felt safe with him, felt that he paid attention to my
weight and to every detail of my health. One day I

waited to go into his office; wearing a blue dress and black tights, I leaned against the wall just outside. He was speaking to a very old woman; she was carefully dressed—we had this in common, to be clean and carefully dressed for our doctor. She said, "I have flatulence. It's so embarrassing. What can I do?"

He shook his head sympathetically. "That's a toughie," he said.

For years, my girls would say "That's a toughie" to something that was a pickle for them—they had heard me tell the story so many times.

I don't know the last time I saw this doctor. I went a few times in the years after my hospital stay, and then once when I called for an appointment they said he had retired and I could see his associate. I could have written a letter to him to tell him what he meant to me, but there were problems in my life and my concentration was not good. I never wrote him. I never saw him again. He was just gone, this dear, dear man, this friend of my soul in the hospital so long ago, disappeared. This is a New York story too.

When I was in Sarah Payne's class, a student from another class came to see her. It was at the end of the class, and people sometimes lingered to speak with Sarah, and this student from the other class came in and said, "I really like your work," and Sarah said thank you and, sitting at the table, began to pack up her things. "I like the stuff about New Hampshire," the student said, and Sarah gave a quick smile and nodded her head. The student said, moving toward the door, as though she would follow Sarah from the room, "I knew someone from New Hampshire once."

Sarah, to my eyes, looked bemused. "Did you," she said.

"Yes, Janie Templeton. You never met Janie Templeton, did you?"

"I never did."

"Her father was a pilot. For the airlines. Pan Am or something it was back then," said this student, who was not young. "And he had a nervous breakdown, Janie's father. He started to walk around their house masturbating. Someone told me that later, that Janie saw this—maybe she was in high school, I don't know, but her father started walking around the house just masturbating compulsively."

I became freezing cold in the Arizona heat. I had goosebumps all over me.

Sarah Payne stood up. "Hope he didn't fly the plane much. Okay, then." And she saw me, and nodded at me. "See you tomorrow," she said.

I had never before heard, nor have I heard since, of this *Thing*—as I had called it to myself—happening as it had happened in our home.

I think it was the next day that Sarah Payne spoke to us about going to the page with a heart as open as the heart of God.

———

Later, after my first book was published, I went to a doctor who is the most gracious woman I have ever met. I wrote down on a piece of paper what the student said about the person from New Hampshire named Janie Templeton. I wrote down things that had happened in my childhood home. I wrote down things I'd found out in my marriage. I wrote down things I could not say. She read them all and said, Thank you, Lucy. It will be okay.

I saw my mother only one time after she came to see me in the hospital. It was almost nine years later. Why didn't I go there to visit her? To visit my father, and my brother and sister? To see the nieces and nephews I had never seen? I think—to say it simply—it was easier not to go. My husband would not come with me, and I didn't blame him. And—I know the defensiveness in this sentence—my parents and my sister and my brother never wrote me, or called me, and when I called them it was always hard; I felt I heard in their voices anger, a habitual resentment, as though they were silently saying *You are not one of us,* as though I had betrayed them by leaving them. I suppose I had. My children were growing, they needed something all the time. My two or three hours a day in which to write were terribly important to me. And then my first book was being readied to publish.

But my mother became ill, and so I was the one, then, who went to her hospital room in Chicago, to sit at the foot of her bed. I wanted to give her what she had given me, the kind of wide-awake constancy of attentiveness of those days she had been with me.

My father greeted me when I stepped off the elevator in the hospital, and I would not have known who he was except for the gratitude I saw in the eyes of this stranger, that I had come to help him. He looked so much older than I had ever thought he could be, and any anger I felt—or that he felt—did not seem connected to us anymore. The disgust I had had for him most of my life was not there. He was an old man in a hospital who had a wife who was going to die. "Daddy," I said, staring at him. He wore a wrinkled collared shirt and jeans. I think he was too shy at first to hug me, so I hugged him, and imagined the warmth of his hand against the back of my head. But in the hospital, that day, he did not, in fact, put his hand across the back of

my head, and something inside me—deep, deep inside—
heard the whisper *Gone.*

My mother was in pain; she was going to die. This
was not something I seemed able to believe. My children were by then teenagers and I was worried especially about Chrissie, whether she was smoking too
much weed. So I was on the phone to them frequently,
and the second evening as I sat near my mother she said
to me quietly, "Lucy, I need you to do something."

I stood and went to her. "Yes," I said. "Tell me."

"I need you to leave." She said this quietly, and I
heard no anger in her voice. I heard her decisiveness.
But truly, I felt panic.

I wanted to say: If I leave, I will never see you again.
Things have been hard with us, but don't make me
leave, I can't bear to never see you again!

I said, "Okay, Mom. Okay. Tomorrow?"

She looked at me, and tears pooled in her eyes. Her
lips twitched. She whispered, "Now, please. Honey,
please."

"Oh, Mommy—"

She whispered, "Wizzle, please."

"I'll miss you," I said, but I was starting to cry, and I
knew she could not stand that, and I heard her say, "Yes,
you will."

I bent and kissed her hair, which was matted from her being sick and in bed. And then I turned and took my things, and I did not look back, but when I stepped through the door, I could not keep walking. I backed up without turning around. "Mommy, I love you!" I called out. I was facing the hallway, but her bed was the closest to me, and she would have heard me, I am sure. I waited. There was no answer, no sound. I tell myself she heard me. I tell myself—I've told myself—this many times.

Immediately I went to the nurses' station. I said, begging, Please don't let her suffer, and they told me they would not let her suffer. I didn't believe them. There had been the woman in the room dying when I was first having my appendix out, and that woman had been suffering. Please, I begged these nurses, and I saw in their eyes the deepest fatigue of people who cannot do any more about anything.

In the waiting room was my father, and when he saw my tears he shook his head quickly. I sat by him and whispered what my mother had said, that she needed me to leave. "When will the service be?" I asked. "Oh, please, tell me when it is, Daddy, I will come right back."

He said there would be no service.

I understood. I felt I understood. "People would

come, though," I said. "She's had those sewing customers, and people would come."

My father shook his head. No service, he said.

And there was no service for her.

Or for him, the next year, when he died from pneumonia; he would not let my brother take him to a doctor. I flew to see him only days before he died, staying in the house I had not seen for so many years. It frightened me, the house, its smells and its smallness, and the fact that my father was so ill and my mother gone. Gone! "Daddy," I said, sitting on the bed by him. "Daddy, oh, Daddy, I'm sorry." I said that again and again: "Daddy, Daddy, I'm so sorry. I'm sorry, Daddy." And he squeezed my hand, his eyes were so watery, his skin so thin, and he said, "Lucy, you've always been a good girl. What a good girl you've always been." I am quite certain he said this to me. I believe, though I am not sure, that my sister left the room then. My father died that night, or rather very early the next morning, at three o'clock. I was alone with him, and when I heard the sudden silence I stood and looked at him and said, "Daddy, stop it! Stop it, Daddy!"

When I got back to New York after seeing my father—
and my mother, the year before—after seeing them for
the last time, the world began to look different to me.
My husband seemed a stranger, my children in their
adolescence seemed indifferent to much of my world. I
was really lost. I could not stop feeling panic, as if the
Barton family, the five of us—off-kilter as we had
been—was a structure over me I had not even known
about until it ended. I kept thinking of my brother and
my sister and the bewilderment in their faces when my
father died. I kept thinking how the five of us had had a
really unhealthy family, but I saw then too how our

roots were twisted so tenaciously around one another's hearts. My husband said, "But you didn't even like them." And I felt especially frightened after that.

My book received good reviews, and suddenly I had to travel. People said, How crazy—such an overnight success! I was on a national morning news show. My publicist said, Act happy. You are what these women who are getting dressed for work want to be, so you get on that show and you act happy. I have always liked that publicist. She had authority. The news show was in New York, and I was not as scared as people assumed I would be. The business of fear is a funny business. I was in my chair, with my microphone attached to my lapel, and I looked out the window and I saw a yellow taxi and I thought, I am in New York, I love New York, I am home. But when I traveled to other cities, as I had to do, I was terrified almost constantly. A hotel room is a lonely place. Oh God it is a lonely place.

This was right before email became the common way for people to write one another. And when my book came out I received many letters from people telling me what the book had meant to them. I received a letter from the artist of my youth telling me how much he liked the book. Every letter I received I answered, but I never answered his.

When Chrissie left for college, then Becka the next year, I thought—and it's not an expression, I'm saying the truth—I did think I would die. Nothing had prepared me for such a thing. And I have found this to be true: Certain women feel like this, that their hearts have been ripped from their chests, and other women find it very freeing to have their children gone. The doctor who makes me not look like my mother, she asked me what I did when my daughters went to college, and I said, "My marriage ended." I added quickly, "But yours won't." She said, "It might. It might."

When I left William, I did not take the money he offered me, or the money the law said was mine. In truth, I didn't feel I deserved it. I wanted only for my daughters to have enough and that was agreed upon right away, that they would have enough. I also felt uncomfortable about where the money came from. I could not stop thinking the word: Nazi. And for myself, I didn't care about having the money. Also I had made money—What writer makes money? But I had made money and I was making more, and so I didn't think I should have William's money. But when I say "And for myself, I didn't care," I mean this: that to be raised the way I was, with so little—only the inside of my head to call my own—I did not require much. Someone else raised in my circumstances would have wanted more, and I didn't care—I say I didn't care—and yet I happened to get money because of the luck I had with my writing. I think of my mother in the hospital saying that money had not helped Elvis or Mississippi Mary. But I know that money is a big thing, in a marriage, in a life, money is power, I do know that. No matter what I say, or what anyone says, money is power.

This is not the story of my marriage; I have said that I cannot write the story of my marriage. But sometimes I think about what first husbands know. I married William when I was twenty years old. I wanted to cook him meals. I bought a magazine that had fancy recipes, and I gathered the ingredients. William passed through the kitchen one evening and looked at what was in the frying pan on the stove, then he came through the kitchen again. "Button," he said, "what's this?" I said it was garlic. I said the recipe called for a clove of garlic to be sautéed in olive oil. With gentleness he explained that this was a bulb of garlic, and that it needed to be peeled and opened into the cloves. I can picture the unpeeled big bulb of garlic now—so clearly—sitting in the middle of the olive oil in the frying pan.

I stopped trying to cook once the girls came along. I could cook a chicken, get them a yellow vegetable every so often, but in truth, food never has held much appeal for me as it does for so many people in this city. My husband's wife loves to cook. My former husband, is what I mean. His wife loves to cook.

The husband I have now grew up outside of Chicago. He grew up in great poverty; at times their home was so cold they wore their coats inside. His mother was in and out of mental institutions. "She was crazy," my husband tells me. "I don't think she loved any of us. I don't think she could." When he was in the fourth grade he played a friend's cello, and he has played with brilliance since. All his adult life my husband has played the cello professionally, and he plays for the Philharmonic here in the city. His laugh is huge, walloping.

He is happy with anything I make for us to eat.

But there is one more thing I would like to say about William: During those earlier years of my marriage he took me to see Yankee games; this was in the old stadium, of course. He took me—and a couple of times the children—to see the Yankees play, and I was surprised at the ease with which he spent the money on the tickets, I was surprised at how he said to go ahead and get a hotdog and beer, and I shouldn't have been surprised; William was generous with his money; I understand that my surprise was because of how it was when my father bought me a candied apple. But I watched those Yankee games with an awe I still remember. I had known nothing about baseball. The White Sox had meant little to me, although I felt a kind of allegiance to them. But after these Yankee games, I loved only the Yankees.

The diamond! I remember being amazed by it, and I remember watching the players hit and run, watching the men who came out to roll the dirt clean, and most of all I remember watching the sun as it set hitting the buildings nearby, the buildings of the Bronx, the sun would hit these buildings, and then different city lights would come on, and it was a thing of beauty. I felt I had been brought into the world, is what I am saying.

Many years later, after I had left my husband, I would walk to the East River by Seventy-second Street, where you can go right up to the river, and I would look up the river and think of the baseball games we had gone to long before and feel a sense of happiness, in a way that I could not feel about other memories of my marriage; the happy memories hurt me, is what I am saying. But the memories of the Yankee games were not like that: They made my heart swell with love for my former husband and New York, and to this day I am a Yankees fan, though I will never again go to a game, I know this. That was a different life.

I think of Jeremy telling me I had to be ruthless to be a writer. And I think how I did not go visit my brother and sister and my parents because I was always working on a story and there was never enough time. (But I didn't want to go either.) There never was enough time, and then later I knew if I stayed in my marriage I would not write another book, not the kind I wanted to, and there is that as well. But really, the ruthlessness, I think, comes in grabbing onto myself, in saying: This is me, and I will not go where I can't bear to go—to Amgash, Illinois—and I will not stay in a marriage when I don't want to, and I will grab myself and hurl onward through life, blind as a bat, but on I go! This is the ruthlessness, I think.

My mother told me in the hospital that day that I was not like my brother and sister: "Look at your life right now. You just went ahead and . . . did it." Perhaps she meant that I was already ruthless. Perhaps she meant that, but I don't know what my mother meant.

My brother and I speak every week on the telephone. He has stayed living in the house we grew up in. Like my father did, he works on farm machinery, but he does not seem to get fired or have my father's temper. I have never mentioned his sleeping with pigs before they are slaughtered. I have never asked him if he still reads the books of a child, those about people on the prairie. I don't know if he has a girlfriend or a boyfriend. I know almost nothing about him. But he speaks to me politely, though he never once has asked me about my children. I have asked him what he knew of my mother's childhood, if she had felt in danger. He says he doesn't know.

I told him of her catnaps in the hospital. Again, he says he doesn't know.

When I speak on the phone to my sister, she is angry and complains about her husband. He doesn't help with the cleaning or the cooking or the kids. He leaves the toilet seat up. This she mentions every time. He is *selfish*, she says. She doesn't have enough money. I have given her money, and every few months she sends me a list of what she needs for the children, although three of them have moved out of her house by now. The last time she listed "yoga lessons." I was surprised that the tiny town she lived in offered yoga lessons, and I was surprised that she—or perhaps it is her daughter— would take them, but I give her the money every time she sends me the list. I resented—privately—the yoga lessons. But I think she feels she is owed the money by me, and I think she may be right. Once in a while I find myself wondering about the man she married, why he never puts the toilet seat down? Angry, says my gracious woman doctor. And shrugs.

In college my roommate had a mother who had not been good to her; my roommate didn't especially like her. But one fall the mother sent my roommate a package of cheese, and neither of us liked cheese, but my roommate could not throw it away, or even stand to give it away. "Do you mind?" she asked. "If we keep this somehow? I mean, my mother gave it to me." And I said I understood. She put the cheese on the outside windowsill and it stayed there, the snow falling on it eventually, and we both forgot about it, but there it was in the spring. In the end she arranged for me to dispose of it when she was in class, and I did.

Let me say this about Bloomingdale's: At times I think of the artist, because he was proud of the shirt he had bought there, and how I remembered thinking that was shallow of him. But my daughters and I have gone there for years; we have our favorite place at the counter on the seventh floor. My daughters and I go first to the counter and have the frozen yogurt, and then we laugh about our stomachs, how much they ache, and then we walk through—so desultory are we—the shoe department, and the department for young women. Almost always I buy them what they want, and they are good and careful and never take advantage—they are wonderful girls. There were some years when they would not go with me, they were angry. I never went to Bloomingdale's without them. Time has gone by, and we go back now when they're in town. When I think of the artist, I think of him with fondness, and I hope that his life has gone well.

But Bloomingdale's—in so many ways—it is home to us, to my girls and me.

Bloomingdale's is home to us because of this: Every apartment I've lived in since I left the home my children grew up in, I have always made sure to have an extra bedroom so they could come and stay, and neither of them ever does or ever did. Kathie Nicely may have done the same, I'll never know. But I've known other women whose children did not visit them, and I've never blamed those children and I don't blame my own, although it breaks my heart. "My stepmother," I've heard my daughters say. "My father's wife" would be sufficient. But they say "my stepmother," or "my stepmom." And I want to say, But she never washed your little faces when I was in the hospital, she never even brushed your hair, you poor little things looked like ragamuffins when you came to see me, and it broke my heart, that no one was caring for you! But I don't say that, and I should not. For I am the one who left their father, even though at the time I really thought I was just leaving *him*. But that was foolish thinking, because I left my girls as well, and I left their home. My thoughts became my own, or shared with others who were not my husband. I was distractible, distracted.

The rage of my girls during those years! There are moments I try to forget, but I will never forget. I worry about what it is they will never forget.

My more tenderhearted daughter, Becka, said to me during this time, "Mom, when you write a novel you get to rewrite it, but when you live with someone for twenty years, that *is* the novel, and you can never write that novel with anyone again!"

How did she know this, my dear, dear child? At such a young age she knew this. When she told me, I looked at her. I said, "You're right."

There was a day late one summer when I was at their father's place. He had gone to work and I was there to see Becka, who was staying, as she always did, with him. He was not yet married to the woman who had brought the girls to the hospital and who had no children of her own. I went to the corner store—it was early morning—and saw on the small television above the counter that a plane had crashed into the World Trade Center. Quickly I returned to the apartment and turned on the television, and Becka sat watching, and I went into the kitchen to drop off whatever I had bought, and I heard Becka cry out, "*Mommy!*" The second plane had gone into the second tower, and when I ran to answer her cry, her look was so stricken: I think always of that moment. I think: This was the end of her childhood. The deaths, the smoke, the fear throughout the city and the country, the horrendous things that have happened in the world since then: Privately I think only of my daughter on that day. Never have I heard before or since that particular cry of her voice. *Mommy.*

And I think sometimes of Sarah Payne, how she could barely say her name that day when I met her in the clothing store. I have no idea if she still lives in New York; she has not written any new books. I have no idea about her life at all. But I think how exhausted she became, teaching. And I think how she spoke of the fact that we all have only one story, and I think I don't know what her story was or is. I like the books she wrote. But I can't stop the sense that she stays away from something.

When I am alone in the apartment these days, not often, but sometimes, I will say softly out loud, "Mommy!" And I don't know what it is—if I am calling for my own mother, or if I am hearing Becka's cry to me that day when she saw the second plane go into the second tower. Both, I think.

But this is my story.

And yet it is the story of many. It is Molla's story, my college roommate's, it may be the story of the Pretty Nicely Girls. *Mommy*. Mom!

But this one is my story. This one. And my name is Lucy Barton.

Chrissie said, not long ago, about the husband I have now: "I love him, Mom, but I hope he dies in his sleep and then my stepmom can die too, and you and Dad will get back together." I kissed the top of her head. I thought: I did this to my child.

Do I understand that hurt my children feel? I think I do, though they might claim otherwise. But I think I know so well the pain we children clutch to our chests, how it lasts our whole lifetime, with longings so large you can't even weep. We hold it tight, we do, with each seizure of the beating heart: *This is mine, this is mine, this is mine.*

At times these days I think of the way the sun would set on the farmland around our small house in the autumn. A view of the horizon, the whole entire circle of it, if you turned, the sun setting behind you, the sky in front becoming pink and soft, then slightly blue again, as though it could not stop going on in its beauty, then the land closest to the setting sun would get dark, almost black against the orange line of horizon, but if you turn around, the land is still available to the eye with such softness, the few trees, the quiet fields of cover crops already turned, and the sky lingering, lingering, then finally dark. As though the soul can be quiet for those moments.

All life amazes me.

Acknowledgments

The author wishes to acknowledge the following for their help with this book: Jim Tierney, Zarina Shea, Minna Fyer, Susan Kamil, Molly Friedrich, Lucy Carson, the Bogliasco Foundation, and Benjamin Dreyer.